Blossom

Angelina Zagonenko

authorHOUSE®

AuthorHouse™
1663 Liberty Drive
Bloomington, IN 47403
www.authorhouse.com
Phone: 1 (800) 839-8640

Published by AuthorHouse 12/20/2017

ISBN: 978-1-5462-2168-5 (sc)
ISBN: 978-1-5462-2169-2 (hc)
ISBN: 978-1-5462-2167-8 (e)

Library of Congress Control Number: 2017919288

Print information available on the last page.

This book is printed on acid-free paper.

Contents

· · · · · · · · · ·

CHAPTER 1

Happy Birthday

· · · · · · · · · · · · · · · ·

Rena looked outside of her school bus window, relieved that she had survived her first week of high school. Everyone had treated her as if she was someone special, like a celebrity, which she couldn't stand. She just wanted to get out of school as quickly as possible. Her thoughts alerted her that one huge gray cloud was approaching covering all that stood in its way. Rena immediately assumed that it was going to rain, and she grabbed her violet-and-blue sweater. Her mother had knitted it for her. They were odd colors, but Rena still loved it and wore it everywhere. The fabric was soft, and it smelled like her mother's perfume. Rena liked her mother's special fragrance. The sweater was like a good luck charm. Every time she wore it, she was reminded of her mother. Her mother was a beautiful woman. She was outgoing, smart, funny, cheerful, and she made a good first impression with everyone she met.

But Rena was the opposite of her mother. She was beautiful, yes, but she never really cared about much. She kept things to herself and was always quiet. The only things she cared about were her three best friends, her little brother, Joey, and her mother and grandparents.

The bus suddenly stopped in front of the stairs leading to her house. Rena's family owned one of the biggest houses in their neighborhood, and Rena didn't like it very much. She hated that her family received so much attention just because her mother was a famous model. She hated that everyone else seemed to like the attention but never really cared about

1

what was really going on. And most of all she hated that she couldn't be a normal girl—that she couldn't walk through the halls at school without everyone looking at her, whispering, and always talking about her mother around her. It was as if they couldn't live their own lives and had to involve their personal matters with hers. Reporters and photographers were often outside her house or school. They would ask her many questions involving her mother. Once a photographer had gone so far as to ask her to tell him about whatever she most wanted to forget about. She threw such a big fit she almost ended up breaking everything in sight. Her mother, of course, didn't mind the attention. Most of the people at her school envied Rena and wished they could live a life similar to hers, but Rena just wanted to escape it all. Rena loved her mother more than anything, but sometimes she just got annoyed about people talking about her. It was as if they couldn't find anything better to talk about.

Rena had only three true best friends. They treated her like a normal high school girl, like a normal person. They didn't care that her mom was a famous model. Still she tried to stay as invisible as possible, which wasn't easy since practically everyone knew her and her family. Eighth grade had been a total disaster, and Rena was hoping this year would be different.

When her family moved from their old neighborhood into this new neighborhood a few miles away from their old one, no one had really payed much attention to them—until her mother insisted that she start a new modeling business and become more of a star than she already was. This made things worse for Rena. Rena wanted to start over. She wondered if moving to a new school would give her a chance to feel like a normal teen.

But no matter what she tried, the second she stepped through the school door, everyone stopped and stared at her. They smiled at her, and Rena just ignored them.

As Rena got off the bus, she heard the bus driver say, "Have a nice day." Rena ignored her and kept walking. As she slowly made her way up the stairs, she watched as one rain drop fell onto the pavement and a dozen more followed right after. Rena looked up the stairs and noticed it was a long walk. She looked at her watch. Three thirty. Her mother would be home shortly. She sighed as she walked up the stairs, finally realizing that she was getting soaked from head to toe.

She quickly held her backpack over her head and ran. When she approached the last step, she noticed that her brother, Joey, was waiting outside, standing in the rain. He was soaking wet. Rena ran up to him. If her mother saw him in the rain like this, she would freak, the smile she tried so hard to keep on would vanish, and Rena would be in so much trouble. But Rena didn't care much what her mother would think. She was more worried about why Joey looked so weird. And why he was standing in the rain without a jacket. His head was down, and his wet hair covered his face.

Rena dropped her backpack and knelt in front of Joey. "Joey, why are you out here? You should be waiting inside where it's warm." But Joey didn't say a word; he just stood there, staring at her. Rena put her hand under his chin and tilted his head up. She noticed that the color of his eyes seemed to be changing, and underneath his eyes were dark circles. The brown in his eyes was being devoured by the red that was quickly seeping in. Rena was a bit frightened by his eyes, which gave her more reason to worry.

She looked at the house, which seemed to be so far away, and then a wave of shock hit her when she remembered about the shed. She turned around and saw the shed next to the stairway. It seemed to be much closer than the house, but Rena had her doubts about it. Still, this wasn't the time for her to have her doubts. They had to get out of the rain. A chilly breeze blew in as the rain poured down. As Rena stood in the rain, she looked at her brother and then made up her mind. Rena grabbed his hand tightly and started running toward the shed. As the rain pierced their skin. Rena saw a bright light near the shed. It glowed brighter as she got closer. Just as Rena thought that light was going to blind her, it suddenly vanished, and Rena was left wondering what it could have been.

As they got closer, Rena noticed that her grasp on her brother's hand tightened, and Joey never complained about it. He was always the kind to whine about such simple things, and sometimes that got really annoying, but Rena had her good times with him, and she enjoyed his company a lot. They were more than brother and sister. Still, Rena wondered why he was acting so weird.

When they arrived at the shed, Rena grabbed the door handle. Her hands were freezing. As she touched the handle, a wave of electricity jolted into her body, shocking her for a second. At the same time, she saw an image. It was a scene of two people. A woman with long red hair was dressed in armor and carrying a long sword at her side. A boy stood next to her. Their faces were blurred. Rena let go of the door handle as if she was paralyzed. She dropped her hand to her side and looked straight at the door. There were very light letters carved into the side of the door, but Rena could not make out the words. The rain dripped from her hair and into her eyes, making her vision blurry.

Rena once again grabbed the door handle. This time she pushed the door open. She quickly rushed in with her brother. She shut the door before the rain entered. As soon as the door closed, they were surrounded in darkness. The shed was shrouded in black. There was no light, only the faint glow from the cracks in the door. But Joey's bright eyes glowed as if filled with evil. "Finally, I have you alone," she heard him say. Rena let go of her brother's hand and turned around to see Joey's eyes glowing much brighter. The red had completely absorbed the brown color she was so used to. His eyes were the color of blood, as if something evil was stirring in him. The light was surprisingly bright, and it revealed what Joey was holding in his hands. Her eyes focused on it—a dagger! It was oddly shaped and looked as if it was made of diamond, and the edges weren't carved smoothly. It might have been a piece of glass, but it looked sharp. Rena tore her gaze away from the dagger and looked up at him, her expression asking him, "What are you doing?"

He showed no emotion. His face was expressionless. Rena looked into his eyes and knew that he was not her brother. Her gaze fell back to the dagger, and Rena was scared out of her mind to think of what he was planning to do.

***

Rena wasn't like most girls. She was tall and beautiful, but also quiet and strange. She hated attention. More than that, her mother was a famous model, and everyone idolized her. She was the one who received the attention of most girls Rena's age. Her mother gave her Rena attention, but the thing was that they couldn't go anywhere alone together without reporters and photographers there waiting, following them. Rena couldn't stand that, so sometimes she gave her mother the cold shoulder.

Rena was also a dreamer. She dreamed that one day all this would disappear. All this fame and fortune, fake friends and popularity. She dreamed that she would become a normal girl, living in a normal neighborhood, going to a normal school, and doing stuff most teens her age would do, not starting her own modeling career. They told her it would be best for her, and Rena agreed, but it was just too much for her to handle. She wanted to do other things kids did, like hang out with friends, go to the pool, walk in the park. Normal things without anyone stopping and staring. She always thought herself to be a strange kid.

When she was just about seven, Rena started telling stories about places she had never heard of. She wasn't into many stories about princesses, but she liked to read many stories about past times. By the time she was thirteen, people enjoyed listening to her stories, and she didn't mind it. She loved it when people sat down and listened to her. She loved that people enjoyed listening to her.

She was hard working and always kept her promises. She mostly liked to keep quiet and stay to herself without telling anyone much. She disliked attention, especially what had happened five years ago. Rena automatically hated attention. Her three best friends were the only three people who treated her the way she wanted friends to treat her. On her second day of school, they came up to her and introduced themselves. They acted perfectly normal around her and never spoke about her mother. It was almost as if they didn't know who she was. They treated her as if she was part of the group, and they gave her no special treatment. And that was when she knew she had found her true friends.

Sometimes Rena would go all out and start acting like a little child, but that only happened for a few seconds. Then she would lose hope again and lock herself up again. But most of the time she was quiet and tried to blend in. Her past revealed a lot about her, but she wasn't that person today. The old Rena vanished inside and refused to come out. She was very responsible and would never back down on her word. She was Rena, quiet but strong. She always found a way to solve her problems. But even at times when things didn't go her way, she tried her best to fix the problem. She was Rena who wanted nothing more than live a normal, quiet life. She was a person who wasn't hard to read, but was not always easy to understand. No one knew what she was going to do next. She was the girl who was just Rena.

***

Joey held the dagger up above Rena's head. It sparkled brightly as the red light fell upon it. Rena wanted to say something, but nothing came to mind. She closed her eyes tightly until she heard Joey speak. "It was hard to find you, but I finally did. Coming to this world wasn't easy." Joey growled, his voice sounded deeper.

"Joey, what are you talking about? You're my brother! You've lived your whole life with me." Rena was frustrated. Why was he holding a dagger above her head? Why was he looking at her with such hatred in his eyes? Why was he making a face as if he was going to kill her?

Rena wanted to close her eyes and think to herself that this was all a dream, something she made up, like one of her school essays, or a creative writing assignment her teacher had given to her. But when Rena opened her eyes, she saw that it wasn't a dream. It wasn't something she had made up right on that spot. It was reality. It was real. Her brother was really holding a dagger above her head!

Rena noticed tears running down her checks. She wiped them away as she looked at her hands. It was as if she saw the reflection of the armored woman she had seen standing with the sword at her side. That women could have given her courage. She found herself saying, "Joey, what are you doing? You've got to snap out of this! Can you hear me?"

"Joey can't hear you anymore. I have completely taken over his body. You are no longer speaking to your little brother."

"What! But how is that possible?" Rena stood their silently, confused about everything that was happening to her right now. She wanted this all gone. She wanted her little brother back. She wished her mother would quickly come home, and all this would be over.

As all of her thoughts clouded her head, she heard her brother speak, but he no longer sounded like her little brother. He sounded so distant, so far away. She heard a quiet voice, as if he was calling out to her, as if it was her brother asking her to save him. It was like a battle between her and the thing that possessed her brother, and Joey was stuck in the middle of it all. It was either them or that beast.

"All things are possible. Now, Sara, I know you can hear me, and I know that you can control this girl, so come with me, or this little boy is coming with me."

Rena's eyes widened. She opened her mouth to say something, but the words that came out of her mouth were not the words she had expected to say. It was as if she was someone else, as if someone else was speaking through her, as if someone was controlling what she said. She felt completely different, isolated. "Do you think this kid really matters to me?" she said. "Do you really think that I will come with you willingly because you're holding a little kid hostage? Please—get real!" she said with a giggle. Rena couldn't believe what she had just said. It was not like her at all. It was as if someone else was inside her body controlling her, controlling her every word. It was as if she was still in her body, but in a different dimension, locked away from her own body. She tried to tell herself, "No, that is not what I wanted to say!" But nothing came out of her mouth.

"You always seemed to care before. I don't think you'd like it if I crushed this boy's soul right here and now." Joey hissed as he walked toward her. Rena wanted to move, but her body refused. She just stood there as Joey came closer.

Then she heard a voice coming from inside of her—the voice that had been speaking to her brother just now. "Do not be afraid!" Rena jerked herself backward, frightened. Her mouth was wide open, and she was breathing heavily. "As I told you before, do not be afraid. I will find a way to get your brother back to you."

"Who are you?" Rena managed to say.

"Well, that's easy—I am *you*! Well, that isn't entirely true. I am a small portion of you—a black pearl hidden deep inside your body."

"And how are you planning to get my brother back?" Rena didn't entirely believe what she'd heard.

"You'll see."

***

Joey was Rena's cute little brother—difficult but sweet. Around the family he acted like a third grader, but when he was around his friends, he acted like kids in the grade he was actually in—fifth grade. He thought that being a fifth grader was the coolest thing ever, and he would always brag to Rena about an assignment he got.

There had always been a special bond between Rena and her brother. They treated each other more like friends than family members—best friends even, as if they couldn't live without one another. Every time Joey felt lonely, Rena would be there. Whenever he was upset or wanted to spend time with Rena, she welcomed him with open arms. They spend a lot of time together, and they didn't argue as much as some siblings did. Sometimes when Rena felt upset, Joey acted like the older brother, asking her to tell him about her problem. He always tried to make her feel better. Sometimes, when he sensed it wasn't a good time, he just left her alone. If their grandparents had been interviewed and asked about them, they would say, "There's never a time when they are not together." Sometimes Joey was a bother and got into trouble, but he was Rena's little brother. What could she expect?

***

Rena's hand moved automatically without her being aware of it. She smiled a thin grin to herself as, out from under her sweater, emerged a long sword. She was struck with surprise as she pulled it out all the way and held it forward with one hand, as if she was going to strike her brother at any minute. "What's going on here?" Rena's voice sounded cracked and she almost couldn't hear herself.

"Don't you worry your pretty head. This will get your brother back."

"But I can't let you do that!" Rena shouted.

"But I have to kill the demon inside of him."

"But you'll hurt my brother!" Rena took control of her arms again. Taking the sword with both hands, she dropped it to the floor. It sounded like a bell when it hit the ground, even though Rena had to use both hands to even barely lift it. "This time I'll do it my way!" She growled, angry at the person inside of her. "You think something like this can control my brother?" she said staring right into her brother's eyes. Her brother walked a little closer, smiling and forcing Rena to back away until she found herself against the door. She looked at her brother, and courage sprang into her heart.

"You don't know one thing about my brother, so how can you possibly be sure you can possess him?"

"I'm in his body right now, am I not?" the beast hissed.

"So what? That doesn't mean anything. Joey is my little brother, and the only people he belongs to are me and my family. I know him better than anyone else. He's stronger than this. He is my little brother, and I know he can get through this. As long as he has friends and a place to come home to, a family that loves him and believes in him, and especially an older sister who loves him and will always welcome him home with open arms. He isn't something you can play with. So you stay out of this!" She shouted as she lifted her hands and stopped the dagger as it was about to slice her. Rena held tight with both hands, focusing all her attention on the dagger. She eliminated everything else in sight and focused only on one thing. No matter what happened, she was going to keep holding until this was all over. She didn't care about anything else. Her mind was totally focused on getting her brother back. She felt her hands getting numb. As the edges of the dagger ripped through her skin, Rena felt warm blood run down her arm. She watched it drip onto the floor and mix with her tears as her brother pushed on the dagger with all his might. Rena lost control of her feet. She fell back, pushing the door open. Light invaded the dark ground. Streams of light shone around the small building. Joey let go of the dagger, and it fell, breaking into a million shards of glass.

Rena noticed Joey falling straight at her. She held out both of her arms and caught her brother. They both tumbled down, but Rena held him close and patted him on the head as she quietly whispered, "Don't worry, Joey. You're with me."

***

"Rena, wake up!" Rena's mom's voice invaded her room. She was shouting for her daughter to get out of bed so she wouldn't be late for school on her very important day. She was probably making bacon with eggs, and she might have burnt it a little. Rena could smell it all the way from the kitchen. It was enough to make her get out of bed. Her mother wasn't always the best cook, yet she always tried her best not to rely on takeout or restaurant food; she preferred homemade.

Rena headed slowly down the stairs. She was tired, but most of all she didn't want to go to school, especially on her birthday. Her mother greeted her from the kitchen. "Good morning, and happy birthday," she said in a sweet voice as she gently kissed her daughter's forehead. Today her mother wore a dark velvet dress that complemented her perfectly, and Rena was happy to see her wear something like that even when she didn't have to go to a photo shoot. That dress looked beautiful on her. Rena was relieved to see her mother wearing something that someone else had not picked out for her. Rena had seen her mother buy that dress herself at the mall one day when they were out shopping. Her mother's long, curly, blond hair tucked beneath her shoulders gave away her charm. Even through Rena had lots of pictures of her mother's photo shoots in her room, she was relieved to see that her mother hadn't fully forgotten about what really mattered.

"I have already baked you a cake, so don't be late coming home from school." Rena's mother smiled, bringing life to her face. Rena hugged her and gave her a weak smile. Instead of eating breakfast, she thought it would be best if she got to school early. She hoped no one would be there. She sat down to put on her shoes. She heard her mother calling out to her grandmother, asking her to get her kimono ready for the Japanese photo shoot that afternoon. Both Rena and her mother were fascinated by the Japanese culture. And it had always been her mother's dream to wear a kimono and go to one of the famous Japanese festivals. Rena was hoping she wouldn't be late for the photo shoot. Her mother had invited her to join her and see how was done. Her mother even promised her she could be in some of the photos with her. Rena was a bit excited about this even though sometimes she couldn't stand to be in the studio during her mother's photo shoots. Still, it was her dream to wear a kimono.

When she walked past the living room, she saw her brother sitting on the couch watching Tom and Gerry cartoons. Rena stood in the door way leaning against the side of the door. "So what's up with this?" she asked him. "Aren't you going to school?"

"No, I'm not feeling very good," he said, turning his head toward her.

"Yeah? Maybe it's an excuse to get out of school?"

"No, I really am sick." he said almost shouting.

Rena turned around. "Yeah? Probably by what happened yesterday." *It's amazing how he can't remember anything*, Rena thought as she looked at her bandaged hands. Her hands still stung, but she didn't mind the pain. She was happy that the voice in her head didn't bother her anymore.

She walked to the front door and opened it wide, but before she left she yelled, "I'm leaving!" And she slammed the door behind her.

As Rena rushed to the stairway, she hoped that the taxi driver wouldn't leave without her. She had always taken the bus, but her mother always had a cab hanging around just in case. It always left at a specific time, and Rena was hoping it hadn't left yet. When she got to the stairs, she suddenly stopped and looked at the shed. Rena knew that going there yesterday had been a mistake and, boy, was she right. She never wanted something like that to happen again. Rena stared at the small building, refusing to move. She was afraid that, if she did, something might happen again. She was afraid about that thing coming and possessing someone else. But Rena had an urge to go closer to shed, even though she knew perfectly well that something bad might happen again. Her parents always kept the shed for storing supplies, and her grandfather mostly used it for his old books.

She was still confused about the voice in her head and how it had controlled her movements. She was also confused about the sword. What was up with that? It looked exactly like the sword she had seen in her vision. Just then, the image popped up in her head. Rena shook it out of her mind and looked straight at the shed. As she got closer, she could feel a chill in the air. The birds weren't singing. Everything was quiet. Something has disturbed the balance of nature.

As Rena slowly walked forward to open the shed, her hand was shaking furiously. Even when she put her other hand on top of the shaking one, it still kept trembling. She heard a loud banging, but Rena did not look away. She felt like running away, but instead she opened the door. To her surprise, she saw Joey standing in the middle of the shed. Rena felt as if she had swallowed her own heart. She froze in fear, her eyes wide in terrier. "Joey," she quietly said, a little scared. She stepped forward, and the door shut behind her. Only a small twinkle light shone. Then it was as if something inside of her had awakened. "I didn't see you come in. Are you feeling all right?" A shadow grew over Joey's face. As he looked down at the ground, he no longer looked like himself. "Joey, are you all right?" Rena shouted, wanting to come closer. But it was as if she couldn't move. Her body refused to move an inch. Her heart started racing. Her thoughts jumped back to yesterday's scene. She didn't want to repeat it again.

"Huh, I knew it. That demon seemed to withdraw pretty quickly without a fight or anything. It was probably lying low waiting for the perfect opportunity." The voice in her head had returned.

Rena opened her mouth to say something, but nothing came out. It was not as if the voice was controlling her body as it had before, but she just couldn't think what to say.

Seconds passed, and she finally gained the strength to say, "Joey, do you remember that it's my birthday?" She gave him a concerned smile as she tried to stay calm as if nothing was wrong. "Remember? Well, I guess you may have forgotten. You've always been a goof ball at that." But Joey didn't say a word. He still stared at the ground. This made Rena more upset, and she wanted him back more than ever. "I always have ... I always have remembered your birthday. It's funny—I always try to be the one to congratulate you first. I remember one time when you looked so happy because you didn't expect it. That's the happiest I have ever seen you. Do you remember that day?" A stream of tears clouded her eyes.

Rena looked at Joey. He held his head down, but she didn't expect to see tears falling onto the floor. "I do remember," he whispered. "You were always there when I needed you. That day you said it—it meant everything to me. How can I ever forget something like that?" The shadow cleared up from his face, and Joey looked at Rena. Rena saw tears in his eyes.

"Joey," she said, running to him.

"Rena I almost forgot to tell you this—happy birthday!"

Rena hugged him. "Joey, you remembered! I'm so happy!" Then something else caught Rena's attention. Something was glowing in the corner of the shed. Rena followed the light, and it led her into another room, which was filled with old boxes stacked up against each other. Old dirty silverware, several lamps, and three boxes of ancient looking teacups were scattered about. She also saw rolls of some old wallpaper that had been used in some of her mother's photo shoots.

Rena was led to the back of the room where she found a stack of papers lying on the floor next to a shelf filled with books. The light faded away as Rena got closer. She lifted up the curtains that covered something as tall as she was. A full-length mirror in a carved stone frame was revealed. Rena watched as the mirror reflected the darkness. Then she saw herself in the mirror. Rena stared at herself. She couldn't believe that it was really her reflection staring right back at her. She looked the same, but she had long red hair, and she was wearing armor. "Amazing," the voice spoke. "The legendary sonic mirror, built almost five thousand years ago, maybe even more. It said that this mirror can show you the future or the past. It's been said that some believe it can travel through time and take you back into the time period when it was created—the place where I used to live." Rena felt her arm lift up. She placed her hand on the stone frame of the mirror. She traced her hand down the frame until her hand hit a carved symbol. As she grasped the symbol, she felt it move, and suddenly everything around her started trembling. The books started falling off the shelves, and the papers flew everywhere. Rena felt as if an earthquake was occurring. She fell to the ground. Finally, the trembling stopped. Rena looked up at the mirror. She thought her eyes might be tricking her as she looked up at what she saw in front of her. In the glass of the mirror she saw a world that was far different from hers. It seemed to be a place she had never dreamed of. She had never known such a place existed. It was a place that was back in time.

"Amazing! So the rumors are true." Rena looked at the mirror carefully. She had never been so fascinated by anything in her entire life. She felt inspired, as if this was a page to a new beginning—a new start in her life, a new chapter in her life story.

But then, hearing the sound of her brother's voice brought her back to reality. "Who would have thought that an old mirror like this would be found in your shed?" Her brother's voice had changed tone; it sounded deeper.

"No! The demon hasn't left your brother's body," the voice said.

How could have I not sensed that? thought Rena. *It's been tricking us this whole time.*

"For a powerful woman, you can be pretty dumb."

"Joey!" Rena shouted.

"Don't waste your energy. You are not speaking to your brother anymore." Rena looked at Joey, disappointed.

"But how?"

"It was simply an act. I used his past memory to trick you." Joey came closer to Rena. He grabbed her arm and pulled her closer. "I just needed you to find the mirror for me so I can return home." Rena swallowed slowly as she listened. She stared at her brother's bright-red eyes. Then he let go of her and pushed her to the ground. He was about to step into the mirror when he stopped and turned to Rena. "Oh, Rena girl, if you ever want to see your brother again, I suggest you follow me. And, Sara, don't think you can escape me." And he was gone. He walked into the mirror and vanished.

Rena got up off the ground and ran to the mirror. She yelled out for Joey, but no one answered. She yelled again and again until her voice was reduced to a whisper.

"He cannot hear you. He might even be on the other side of the mirror."

"But I can't just leave him!" she shouted, turning around and finding no one there.

"Then we must go into the mirror."

Rena turned back to the mirror. "You mean go in there?" She looked at the mirror's reflection. She touched the reflection with one finger, and it rippled as if it was made of water. "No way I'm going in there!" She swallowed hard and looked back at the shelf of books. She picked up some of the fallen books and put them back on the shelf.

"Look, do you want to save your brother or not?" she heard the woman shout.

"I do!" Rena shouted back.

"Then go into the mirror. This is no time to hesitate. He could be in grave danger, and you're the only one who can save him—with my help of course." Rena looked back at the mirror and again swallowed the lump in her throat. She imagined her brother, Joey, in a different world—a strange place that he knew nothing about. She imagined him all alone and scared. She remembered what it was like to be his age. Joey might have been years younger than she, but he had always been there for her. He had always waited for her after school. And after Dad died, and he found her crying, he would be the only one who would comfort her, the only one who could make her feel better. She couldn't just leave him alone. Rena reached one hand out toward the mirror as if someone would grab it, and she stepped into the shimmering image.

CHAPTER 2

The Other Side of the Mirror

• •

Rena closed her eyes for a while, but then she opened them. Lights of all different colors were flashing around her. Several more mirrors stood in front of her, and she passed right through them. The lights flashing by her seemed magical—time-traveling magic. The glow of dashing, wonderful colors flew right by her. She felt as if she was flying though time, going back so many years. In front of her still stood the scenery. It seemed to be waiting for her to jump into its mythical power so it could engulf her with the first breath of the new world that lay ahead. Everything was going to change in her life one step at a time. Rena felt as if the sun's rays were already touching her, surrounding her with bright warm light.

Before now, Rena had never imagined something like this was possible. She never imagined that she would be traveling through a mirror to a different dimension, a different world that she knew nothing about. She especially never imagined she would be traveling to save her beloved brother from the demon that had possessed him. She never could have imagined that something like this was real, that it was possible.

At last Rena entered into the world she had been telling people about all her life, but never really believed in herself. It was a world filled with magic and power, but also danger and destruction. The light in front of her suddenly illuminated all that was around her. She was inside the mirror, and nothing stood between her and that vivid world that stood before her, waiting for her to step out of her shell and feel the wonders of the new world.

She stepped one foot out of the mirror as she watched the image in front of her with her dark eyes. She wanted to grab the image and hold it in her hands as if the world was a tiny glass ball and she was its protector, but instead she found herself at the bottom of a hole. Rena quickly looked around her. Aware of her situation, she quickly tried to find something to climb on, but she could see nothing useful in this solitary place. Rena looked up and saw a small light above her. How much she wanted to reach for that light, to take a hold of it, to grab on to that last strand of life. She stretched her hands out as if she would grab that flaming ball of light. Her hands closed in on the light, only to disappoint her.

Coming down to the most logical explanation she had, she called out to the voice in her head. "Hey, Sara, help me out here!"

"Sorry, kiddo. You must find your own path to climb."

"Now you decide not to offer advice! Some help you are." She still did not believe that she was talking to a voice inside her head. She stopped at her words and smiled. Rena looked around her. It looked as if she was stuck in time. She seemed to be in a black hole at a bottom of a well, and the only way out was up. There were no walls, only darkness. Rena walked up against one of the walls and put one ear to the blackish surface, but she didn't hear anything. This bottomless pit was starting to frighten her, and she wished she could get out of it as quickly as possible. She circled the dark pit several times. Stopping, she stomped one foot in anger. She screamed and cried at the chamber that held her captive. But when she did that, nothing happened. Then she focused her attention. She tried to remember what her grandfather had told her and what he had written in one of his books, all of which were based on his adventures: "When it seems that there is no way out, just close your eyes and think. The answer will come to you shortly." She froze and closed her eyes tightly and listened carefully as she tried to think, tried to figure something. "Be steady and quiet. Feel the energy flow into you. Listen to the sound of water, and feel what you could not feel before."

Suddenly her eyes flew open, and Rena knew what she was going to do next. With luck on her side, she hoped it would work. She pulled from her back jeans pocket a piece of rope, and she tested it to make sure that it was strong and would not break. She tied it around her wrist and then reached into the left side of her jacket. Her hand touched something cold and metallic. She smiled to herself as she pulled out the sword. She tied the other end of the rope to the sword handle and then pitched it forward. And as she had hoped, the sword stuck onto the wall. Rena knew that there was a way out. Finally, she would be out of the dark and into the sunlight. She felt that she wasn't alone, as if someone was watching her—someone with great power, someone who gave a new meaning to the word *frightening*, someone whose presence just gave her the chills.

Rena grasped the rope with both hands and started pulling herself upward, bracing her feet against the rough walls. Suddenly, Rena felt a cold, sharp weight pulling her down. As she looked down at her legs, she saw the most monstrous creature she had ever seen in her life. It was slimy and smelled of burnt rubber, as if it had faced a long and troublesome journey. Her thoughts were scattered, but soon the pain in her legs brought her back to reality. Rena used all her strength to hold herself along with the weight of the creature on the rope until every fiber in every muscle in her arms gave in.

The agonizing pain struck Rena as she fell to the ground, but she knew that she should be more worried about the monster in front of her than she was about the fall. As she came to her senses, the smell of burnt rubber grew stronger, and Rena could feel the close presence of this new enemy. Looking around, Rena became confused. Where had it gone? Just as she used her weak arms to pick herself up, surprise overwhelmed her as she felt the creature's venomous pincers trying to attack her ankles. That's when she clearly saw the creature that had attacked her. It was a giant centipede—the most monstrous creature she had ever seen. She thought—she hoped— that her eyes might be deceiving her. She knew the creature could sense the fear and anger boiling in her veins. Rena looked around and realized she had nowhere to run. She backed away from the centipede, as the giant arthropod slithered closer. As she was tangled up in confusion and fear, she suddenly noticed her brother in the corner, watching.

"Joey!" Rena shouted, happy to see him. But his red eyes seemed to speak for him, and Rena knew that she was no longer talking to her little brother. "I don't get it, Joey. Why are you letting this demon possess you?" she shouted in pain as tears escaped. She reached her hand out to Joey as if he was going to run for it. Instead, a surprising bright-blue glowing light shot out of her hand at Joey. The creature that stood before her slithered to Joey and got in front of him, blocking the blow. It screeched, making a terrifying noise.

"I have plans for this kid, Sara. And I'm not going to let you ruin them." The centipede demon looked at Joey. "I expect you to follow me." Joey nodded. He grabbed something in his hands, and it seemed to lift him up. The centipede was consumed by the depths of an oversized crack in the wall.

After many moments of confusion, Rena snapped back to the bottomless abyss. She remembered what the centipede had said to Sara. "So it was you! You tried to harm my brother again!" She was angry at Sara for being so heartless at times.

"No, this time it was not my doing. It was all you."

"But why would I want to hurt my own brother?"

"I do not know. But quickly start climbing before your brother gets out."

Rena looked up and saw her brother halfway up. She gained her strength and continued to climb up the rope. She grasped the edge of the sword with her shaky hands and pulled herself forward, doing her best to maintain her balance. The familiar ache in her arms had returned. She looked up at her brother and saw that he was already climbing out. She shouted for him, but he did not answer. After what seemed like hours, the unmistakable beam of sunshine and grassy smell reminded her of the perfect summer day she had left for twenty minutes in the dark hole. She finally reached the top, and a beam of light hit her face. She was happy to be outside in the warm fresh air. Surprise overwhelmed her when she saw tall green grass and oak trees as tall as skyscrapers, which were scattered across the field.

As Rena was becoming more aware of her surroundings, she noticed perfect spherical bushes aligned in a straight line as if someone had planted them on purpose. Looking around, Rena couldn't help but notice a flower patch growing nearby. All of the flowers were different colors and looked as if they had been painted by an artist. Everything around her was magical, as if it had been painted with a magical brush. The sunlight—the beam of light that she had longed to feel—surprised her. It rained down, warm, into her hair and spilled upon her checks. The air seemed to be so refreshing, so breathtaking, so cool and warm at the same time. It was as if she was drinking a cup of life's water.

It was a forest unlike any she has seen back home. She had never seen anything similar to it. Nothing even compared to what she was seeing. The experience was something she just couldn't explain with words. A light ocean mist spread throughout the forest, but then it vanished as soon as it had appeared. The nourishment of the lush forest brought life and sound to every plant and animal. Everything Rena heard and saw belonged to a creature of nature. She was mystified by this scene and realized that she had lost all her previous mingled emotions. She was impressed at seeing such a sight. Everything was so beautiful, so refreshing. The impression almost made her feel at home. Everything she saw and touched gave her a new meaning.

Moments later, as she was being magically blown away by the scenery in front of her, her mind brought her back to her real problems. She was surprised to see Joey leaning on one of the trees in front of her, smiling as if he was enjoying this magical place as well. Rena closed her eyes as if she had seen a ghost. When she opened them again, Joey was gone. Rena ran up to the place where she had seen him standing.

But it was as if no one had stood there in the first place. And Rena couldn't sense anyone's presence. Could have she imagined it all? Surprise overwhelmed her as, suddenly, she felt needles piercing her skin. Something grabbed her legs and hauled her back with great strength. Rena felt as if her stomach was being twisted. She was hauled back and forth several times before blood started spewing out of her mouth. At last the agonizing pain stopped, and she was put onto the ground. Her legs were torn with wounds so deep, she believed it would take years for them to heal. Finally catching her breath, Rena caught a glimpse of her attacker. It was Joey. He was holding a very long, like of a snakes skeleton sword as he looked at her. Rena thought to herself that this was not Joey's doing. He was under a spell, being controlled. He would never do something like this to her. Still looking at him, she was in shock, and she couldn't believe that this was her brother.

Rena felt her strength disappearing. She had to do something before she fell into a dreamless sleep. Rena felt a cry escape her lips as Joey's sword came back for more of its victim's blood. Then she heard it—Sara's voice: "Pull out *your* sword! Do it before it's too late!"

Joey's sword was inches away from her when she reached into her sweater and pulled out her own long sword. She was amazed because she hadn't taken it with her when she left the bottomless pit. Rena used her weak hands to pull the sword above her to shield her from Joey's attack. Joey's sword struck her own sword with such a great force that Rena felt the ground tremble. Then she felt the strength within herself. Rena got up. She was barely able to hold herself up. The pain she felt threatened to take her down. She managed to swing the sword as Joey was aiming his sword at her. Her sword cut the end of Joey's blade off. Joey retreated, but before he ran away, he managed to wound Rena's shoulder pretty badly, even with his broken sword.

Rena held one hand to her shoulder and held the other one out as if to grab her brother and pull him close to her. But he only vanished in the daylight. After many minutes in pain, Rena started walking forward, hoping to see her brother again. As she walked, the scent of flowers mixed in with the scent of her blood. Her crimson blood fell, mixing in with the scarlet red of the flowers in a nearby patch. Her sweater was ripped through, and blood was gushing out of her wound. She felt dizzy, and her body ached all over. Her bandaged hands were soaked in her blood. She felt that her feet would give out any minute. She felt that she had no more strength to hold herself upright. She had no strength to fight. She walked farther away from the mirror and sat down. She took off her sweater and put it on her wounded legs, hoping that it would stop the bleeding and ease her pain a little. The blood stained her clothes. The smell around her no longer seemed pleasant. The smell she disliked so much was filling up her nostrils, making her feel light-headed.

Rena got up and walked along, hoping to find some help. Finally, after walking for quite a few minutes, wondering when this nightmare was going to be over, she came upon a tree. Her scattered thoughts raced back until she remembered the old tree in front of their house. She could see it from her damaged old window that needed repairing. She smiled as she remembered that tree. The memory made her feel at home. She felt some of her stress leave her as she looked at the old tree. She wanted to walk closer to it and lie down, get some rest, and dream of the happy days she'd had with her brother. She walked slowly forward, making her way through the line of bushes. As she got closer, the tree seemed to be growing bigger with every step she took. What she saw next gave her the chills. As she came closer to the tree, she looked up and saw someone lying on one of the branches. It was a boy. His hands were tucked behind his head as if he was taking a nap. His hair was silvery white, and the sun's rays made it sparkle. It was beautiful, and Rena believed she had never seen anyone like him. She was amazed and wondered at the way he slept. His skin was so pale and smooth. He looked peaceful. His hair looked real and original, which made her want to touch it.

Rena climbed into the tree, trying to get close to the branch he slept on. His clothes didn't look much different than what she and her brother would usually wear at home. Looking at him almost made her feel at home, as if her worries had been put into a bubble and blown far, far away. She felt that he might be a piece of home. Rena reached one hand out to touch the boy. Suddenly, his eyes flew open. He grabbed Rena's hand tightly. Getting off the branch, he pulled out a small sword. He brought Rena to her knees and held the blade close to her neck. "Who are you?" he said angrily, catching her off guard. She grew weak. She could tell that he wasn't very happy to see her. She felt her strength fading away quickly. Her vision failed her. She fell, and the edge of the sword scraped her neck.

***

As she jolted awake, Rena felt pain in her legs. She held her head high enough to see that she and the boy were now in a small house, and the boy was treating her wounds. She was relived and happy that she had found help, and it had come just in time because she had been about to collapse. She was so happy that she wasn't thinking at all. Then she felt the boy touch her, and it gave her a tingly sensation. Her feet stung as he poured something on them. "Ow!" she cried. But he did not look up at her. Instead he poured more of that stuff, which stung even more. *Rude much?* Rena thought as she lay back down. But she felt grateful because, if it hadn't been for him, she would have— She didn't want to think about what could have happened to her if she hadn't found help in time. In this place, anything was possible.

The wounds in her legs still stung after a while, and it looked as if it would be getting dark soon. The boy walked back and forth without saying a word. Why did he need to, she was just a lost girl, and he was a boy who had been was passing by. He didn't know her, and she didn't know him. Yet he could say something. She felt like saying something, but felt his glare like daggers and just lay there silently. The shadows that were dancing around the window told Rena the sun was setting. How long had she been there?

Rena tried to get up, but the pain forced her back down. She saw the boy walk past her and wondered about him. "What are you doing?" she asked, trying to be polite.

"Mind your own business," he said in a rude way.

Rena felt anger setting in. She counted to ten, and then her anger evaporated. But when he looked at Rena the expression he gave her suggested that he had just realized that he was talking to a girl. It was as if, for some reason, he had just noticed that she was there. It was as if he didn't even know he had helped her. She wondered if he had been unconscious the whole time. He looked at her in sort of a polite way, but then, as quickly as it had come, his expression changed, and he quickly looked away. The boy opened the door, but just before he left, he looked back at Rena. "Don't leave! Got that?" he said in a grumpy voice, causing Rena to become even angrier at him. But then she reminded herself that he was the one who had saved her, and he had even treated her wounds. He didn't have to, but he had helped a complete stranger. Yet he was acting so rudely.

She just flashed him a smile. He rolled his eyes and walked away. Even though she didn't like it, she knew that the polite thing to do was just to stay quiet and do what the boy had asked. Even though he had spoken to her rudely and he had, at one point, looked at her as if she was someone he couldn't care less about, his eyes now looked at her differently—in a sweet and caring kind of way. When he looked at her, she felt as if her heart was melting. Even though he wasn't polite, he was handsome. He looked so calm. She admired his beautiful amber eyes and short white hair. He had a sort of "bad boy" attitude about him, and that's what made her heart race so fast.

Rena tried to rest, but all her emotions made her jumpy. She couldn't relax no matter how hard she tried. She no longer felt the sting in her legs, and she noticed the wind outside had grown stronger, and the sky had darkened. She was starting to get worried about the kid, and she wondered where he had gone. She thought that maybe she should go look for him. But then she thought about what he had told her, and she decided that what he did was none of her business. But she no longer felt the pain, and that gave her the perfect excuse to go look for him.

CHAPTER 3

Smells Like Trouble

· · · · · · · · · · · · · · · · · ·

What was she doing? Going out at this late hour, when it was storming outside, and when she was badly hurt; looking for someone who had given her a not-so-welcome reception and treated her like she was invisible. She had more important things to do then run after some boy who had acted like a total jerk to her. Still she had to do this, to thank him for what he had done for her. This was the only way she knew how to do it.

She shivered as she walked forward and noticed the she wasn't wearing her sweater, only her tank top. And her stomach was bandaged. She smiled as she thought of him. Then she turned her head to look back and noticed that she didn't know where to go and that she was far from the house.

Suddenly Rena smelled something. It smelled like smoke. Lunging forward, she ran to place she thought it was coming from. Even though the boy might not be there, she needed to know what had caused that smoke. If anyone was in trouble, she would help. Just when she passed the last of the oak trees, she saw him. The sky roared above her as the wind blew her hair forward. It was pitch black outside, but Rena could see what was in front of her. The kid was lying on the ground, unconscious, and a demon panther stood next to him blowing fire from its mouth. Rena felt her heart lunge forward as she froze in her tracks. She wanted to shout out, but something stopped her. What was this? Sure, this time period she'd landed in might be thousands of years back, but she never expected to see something like this.

Rena stood in the same exact spot for a few seconds, not moving. When she finally broke free from her trance, she yelled out to the boy as she ran forward, pulling out her sword and standing right in front of him. She had to do something—anything. She tried to search deep inside of herself for the powers that had been closed in for so long. Wait, what was she thinking? The only power she had was the sword, and that was from Sara. It wasn't even her own power, and she shouldn't even be thinking about this.

Just then, the voice of the panther demon distracted her from her thoughts, and she soon focused on the more important problem she was facing at that time. "Girl, what do you think you are doing? Get out of my way or I will burn you alive!" the panther hissed. Rena was amazed. That thing could talk!

"You think I'm going to let you kill him? A weak thing like you?" Rena stopped herself before she went any further with her words. She couldn't believe what she was saying. She wasn't thinking at all. It wasn't like her at all. Maybe the old Rena would say something similar, but not this new Rena. Or maybe it was Sara again. She and Sara did share the same body, and the old Rena did think a lot like Sara. What was she thinking? This wasn't the time or place to think something like that.

"I'm going to enjoy ripping your throat out." The panther demon walked into the open and stared down at Rena. Then the demon blew fire at her. Rena used her sword to shield her from the attack. Then she heard his voice again. "What are you doing? Didn't I tell you to not leave the house? Leave! I can take care of this myself." He struggled to get up.

"No!" Rena shouted back.

"Look, Zidika, you're not okay. Just lie back down, and I will take care of this." Before she had finished speaking, his head dropped to the ground.

Rena looked for an opening. After she found one, she ran forward. With a swoop, a rush of bright and beautiful colors tangled into one and swirled around together creating one massive vortex of energy that headed toward the demon. Within seconds, the demon was completely consumed by the light full of colors. Rena had never seen anything like that, and as soon as it had disappeared, she stared up at the sky as if it might appear once more just for her.

Rena was so happy as she looked back to the boy and gave him a bright smile full of love, joy, and hope. For a second she had forgotten about everything. But then she remembered what was going on. When she saw him give her a cold stare, she started running to him. Her brown eyes met his amber eyes for a second. Just then the coldness in his eyes disappeared, and he looked at her as if he knew her. She looked like someone he had known and loved a long time ago, but it couldn't be her—it must be someone else, this girl who didn't seem to want to leave him alone, who clung to him like a puppy.

Rena ran up to him and helped him up. At first, he moaned, but he said that he would be okay on his own. But when he tried to support himself on his own, Rena saw how much trouble he had. Ignoring the familiar glares he gave her, she placed his arm around her shoulders. He supported himself a bit. Rena felt the sting in her legs as she supported him.

They walked slowly back to the house trying not to tip over. Rena tried her best to not let go. She also tried not to feel the pain.

He could feel her doing her best to not fall and not cry so pathetically. She wanted to show him that she was strong, that she wasn't some weak girl he'd just met and immediately thought that she was useless. She had trouble walking, and he knew that, but only one thing was on his mind.

"How do you know my name?" he asked her. He had never told her his name, and wasn't even planning to, yet somehow she already knew it.

Rena looked at him then said, "I don't know. It just came to me as if it was the right thing to say."

Zidika did not react. He tried his best to support himself, but all attempts were in vain, and he ended up putting his head on her shoulder. Rena looked at him and noticed that his eyes were barely open. She smiled.

As they walked back to the house Rena, could tell that it was going to rain. She knew that the house was too far away, and they wouldn't reach it before the rain started. So she went off the path. Seeing a cave nearby, she started walking to it. She felt happy—a ridiculous kind of happy. She was happy in a giggly kind of way that made her want to scream with joy. It made no sense. She had never been this happy about something, and it all seemed so silly. She knew that other girls sometimes felt that way, but why her? Why did she feel this way?

This place—it was as if it was changing her. She needed help. What was happening to her? What was he doing to her? What was this place doing to her? A day that was supposed to be one of the worst was actually turning out to be fine! Ever since she met him—this Zidika kid—she hadn't been thinking much about her brother, and her angry feelings seemed to be slowly evaporating into the air.

And the craziest part about all this was that emotions were stirring up inside her. They were the kind she thought she would never have, and it made her feel like a carefree kid.

She was frustrated and angry. How could he do this to her? Turning her to mush, making her do and say things she'd never cared about or wouldn't think to do. Making her care for him so much that it felt as if her heart was a piece of glass and would break if he said anything to her. She was mad at him for making her like this.

She realized that her quiet self—the girl who hated attention—was leaving her, and the crazy outgoing girl was starting to come inside to take her rightful place. She told herself that she was doing this for him because he had helped her and she was repaying him. Nothing else. There was no other reason. The fact that she let him lie against her shoulder was weird. And he didn't seem like the kind of guy who would allow himself to do something like that. She felt strange inside, yet it felt good.

***

Her skin was soft and warm. Since she had nothing on but her tank top, he could feel how soft her skin was and how sweet she smelled. Even with the cold air blowing, she felt warm, and he wanted it to stay that way. This girl was so gentle and fragile, like a piece of thin glass that could shatter at any given moment. He felt that about her.

He had never trusted anyone, but for some reason this girl was different. It wasn't as if he hadn't ever seen a girl before. But she had the most adorable smile. And he felt he could drown in her dark-brown eyes. He trusted her to take care of him, at least for the night until he felt better. Why did he trust her? He didn't know why.

Even though she smelled good, he could sense that she was trouble, and he did not like that. She smelled like trouble no matter how good that fragrance was. She was in trouble. She had a problem. That was why she had come to him. She had not admitted it. He knew it. That was the only explanation for her behavior, the wounds in her legs, and how badly her shoulder was hurt. She had helped him when he was in trouble only because she wanted his help. But what amazed him more was how she'd been able to pull out that sword.

Still she had a problem that needed solving. He usually never got involved with people's problems. He would send people away who asked him to slay a demon for them. Why should she be any different? This girl was going to cause problems for him, and he had enough problems on his own to deal with. He didn't need any more trouble. He had enough enemies, and with a girl like that, things would just get more difficult for him. She had trouble written all over her. He was just going to leave her before she brought up the question—before she has a chance to ask him.

He had always been on his own. Why should things change? Why would he allow himself to help her when he had sent so many others away? He was angry at himself for letting her possess him, letting himself be caught in her deadly web.

As he thought about always being alone, something flashed into his head— the image of a long-haired woman's face. Then he remembered that he hadn't always been alone. At one time, he did have someone by his side. But she had left him, and that was when he swore he would never let anyone close to him again. This girl looked so much like that woman, and when she spoke, her words were similar to what the woman might have said.

For some strange reason, however, he thought this girl was different. Unique. He had let her get close to him, hold him, touch him. He had allowed himself to help her, and now he was stuck and didn't know how to get out of it.

Why would a girl go out of her way to help him? Especially when she could barely hold herself up! He was tired from all this thinking. It made him dizzy, and he wanted to rest. He closed his eyes for a little while—just a little—to clear his head.

CHAPTER 4

Lost

· · · · ·

Maybe he should stop pretending to be asleep. What had gotten into him? Why was he acting like this? She was quite similar to every other girl he had met, even though she might be a little different. It didn't matter. He was acting strange around her, and he could not understand why.

Just as he was about to move over to let the girl know he was awake, he felt his head kneeling. Now he was totally awake. He stole a glance at her through his eyelashes. He was confused and unsure about what to do. She looked as if she might have been sleeping, but then she opened her eyes and lifted her head up and looked around. He was lying with his head on her lap. She looked around and seemed frightened, as if she expected someone to jump out from behind a rock and attack them. But then she relaxed herself and started breathing normally. He closed his eyes and tried to rest, because for some reason he felt terribly weak and felt as if he couldn't get up. Suddenly a warm and gentle hand touched his forehead. What was she doing? Then suddenly she pulled her hand back. He heard her gasp and wondered what was wrong.

"You have a fever," she said softly, but she wasn't sure he heard her because he was still pretending that he was asleep.

Rena looked around the place to see if there was anything she could use to cushion Zidika's head while she went to get water. She found a pile of sticks. Rena placed Zidika's jacket on the pile of sticks and then she carefully placed his head down. When he was settled, she left. When she returned, she had a piece of cloth and a bowl of water, which she she set near Zidika. She placed the cool, wet cloth on his head. After a few minutes, she removed it and wet it again in the cool water. "My brother often got sick with a fever, and I often took care of him," she said so softly. She placed one hand on his head and brushed his bangs from his face. Her gentle hands took care of him. He trusted her to take care of him. She acted as if she was taking care of a kid, a baby, a fragile thing that could break. Even her speech was soft and gentle, just like her hands. Then she hummed a quiet melody. It seemed to sound familiar, but he couldn't think of where he might have heard it. It soothed him and comforted him, and now he really did fall asleep.

Rena had finally finished everything she needed to do. Why was she doing this? She didn't know. Maybe it was because he reminded her of her brother. The thought never hit her that she was repaying him. She just wanted to do this. For him. She lay down a few feet away from him close to the fire she had built. Now all she had to do was survive the night.

***

The sound of birds chirping and singing a lovely melody woke Zidika from a dream of grassy fields and beautiful flowers that smelled so fine. He opened his eyes and stood up. By the height of the sun, he could tell that it was probably eight o'clock. He felt much better. He was still a little dizzy when he stood up, but at least he didn't have a fever. He was about to put on his jacket when he noticed Rena sleeping nearby. Was this the girl who had taken care of him? The girl who had sung a beautiful song? The girl whose hands were so warm and gentle? The girl who felt so warm and nice? The girl who looked so much like the woman he remembered? Was she really that girl? The girl he had helped? The girl he had saved? The girl that … what were the word? She was sweet, gentle, caring, and what was the last word? What was the last syllable he wanted to say? Looking at her, he had forgotten what he wanted to say. There were no words to describe the way she was sleeping like an innocent baby, expecting him to take care of her.

He walked over to the girl and put his jacket around her shoulders. She looked peaceful and relaxed. She looked so much like the woman he remembered—so beautiful, yet dangerous. He couldn't let this happen again. He didn't want it to happen. He was not going to let it happen.

He remembered the first time they had met. He thought he was being attacked. He didn't know how to respond to that. He smiled as he remembered that thought. He started slowly walking away from the cave.

***

By the time Rena woke up it had been drizzling a little. But the sun's rays had recently broken through the raindrops and were now shining into the cave, making the morning even more beautiful. Rena opened her eyes feeling relaxed and refreshed. She was so happy that the morning was so beautiful. This was something she would never see at home. Birds would be singing outside her window, but when she looked outside, all she would see were huge buildings. Here, it was a different story. Nature was everywhere, and there were no buildings or other modern things she always encountered in her world. She was happy that she had slept so comfortably. She was warm too. Warm?

Rena looked around her and realized that Zidika's jacket was around her shoulders. The last time she'd seen it, it was serving as a pillow for Zidika's head. How had it ended up on her? Maybe, just maybe, he had put it on her when she was sleeping. Maybe he wasn't such a bad guy after all. She picked up the edge of his jacket and sniffed it. For some strange reason she wanted to. It smelled like him. It smelled good—like dirt and the fresh air. She didn't know if she should be happy or thankful.

He was behind her carrying a pile of sticks. He watched as Rena examined his jacket. He did not know what to say or what to do, so he just stood behind her until she noticed he was there.

Rena looked around for Zidika and saw him behind her. A red blush stained her face as she stared up at him. Had he seen her? Everything she'd done? Wait, she hadn't done anything wrong, so why was she blushing

34

so hard? And why was he standing in front of her like that? It irritated her and made her mad. He was just standing there watching her and not saying a word. Why was he watching her like that? It frustrated her. She wanted him to leave. She stood up so suddenly that it surprised the boy. His amber eyes looked at her.

"What!" she stared at him, giving him a look that sort of irritated him. Why did he feel that way? No, why was she acting like that? Soon she looked away. She walked up to him and handed him his jacket. She did not say a word; she just slowly started walking away.

Zidika looked at her with a confused expression. Wait, what had just happened? He didn't want her to leave. "Wait!" Zidika lunged forward, grabbing her arm. Rena felt a chill as she turned around. "Won't you have fish first?" Rena looked at the fire and then smiled to herself. She sat down close to the fire, but kept her distance from Zidika. If she sat near him, she would be tempted to ask him, and the last thing Rena wanted to do was get him involved in her problems. She needed help. She needed to find someone who would help her. She always thought she would never be alone, but now she was totally alone. She needed to grow up and solve her own problems. She didn't want to cause any more problems than already existed. Zidika was the last person she wanted to involve. That was why she had been planning to leave in the morning—so she wouldn't burden him with her problems. The thought saddened her.

Zidika had been cooking his fish over the fire. He handed one that was ready to Rena. They both ate in silence. Zidika noticed that the girl tried her best to keep herself apart from him, but, despite her best efforts, she kept glancing at him. She was strange. His ordinary boring day had turned into a strange but exciting day. Zidika watched her from the corner of his eye. Since she did not say anything, he wasn't going to either. He thought that she wouldn't ask him for his help. Besides he was lost in thought about something. *Who is this girl? Where has she come from? She does not exactly fit in around here. Her tank top and jeans look awfully strange to me. Perhaps my clothes look strange to her. She is unfamiliar to me, yet I feel as if I know her.*

Rena looked at him. He was watching her with a strange look on his face, as if he was in deep thought about something. Yet he looked at her as if he knew her. Why? She has never met him before. So why did he look at her as if he knew her? As if maybe he had feelings for her?

"Thank you for the fish," Rena said but she hasn't fully finished it yet.

"No problem. In return for what you did for me, I should be doing more for you than just giving you fish."

A thin smile grew on her face. Rena tried her best not to blush, but it spread across her face anyway. "If I hadn't come, then you would—" but she stopped herself at the thought.

"You practically saved my life twice. Why would you care for someone like me?"

"I don't … I mean I do … It's just … Stop making me confused!" she said, a little sarcasm in her voice. She smiled. This made her feel better.

Zidika watched her as she changed colors, from pale white to red and then green. It amused him.

Rena blew a piece of hair out of her face and said, "I wanted to thank you for what you did." She stood up, brushing the dust of her jeans. She wanted to stay longer but knew she couldn't. But this little chat with him had made her feel better—a lot better. "Thank you for the meal, but I must take my leave." She turned to walk away, but Zidika stopped her.

"Would you tell me your name?" he asked.

Rena turned around, but couldn't even look at him in the eye. Why would he need to know her name when they were leaving each other anyway, for good? "Why?" she said as turned away. "It's not as if we'll ever see each other again." She ran away before he could see the tears in her eyes.

Why did her departure tear at his heart? He should feel relieved. She was a problem. He should be happy to get rid of her. Who is happy to get a problem? Then why did he want that troublesome girl to come back? He should just walk away, never look back, and never think about her again. He should lose the emotions he felt and forget about everything. He felt miserable. She made him feel miserable. How did she make him feel so miserable? He was alone. He had been alone for such a long time that, when she came, he wanted her to stay. At first she seemed like any other person, but then something about her just lightened his day. He felt good just talking to her. He didn't mind her being around. He wanted to be near her. It hurt knowing that he wouldn't be able to see her again. *Look away*, he told himself. *Keep walking and don't look back.*

***

Rena made sure she was far enough away that she could not see the cave. She came to a tree, and she hugged it tightly. *Why did I do that? Why couldn't I just ask him? I know what I said. I know I didn't want to get him involved, but …* She sat against the tree. *Now I will never find Joey.* This was harder than she thought. This was not going as she had planned. She hadn't known that, if she left, she would want to see him again. It surprised her that she had finally gathered enough courage to leave, even though she wanted to stay, and she was also surprised that he had let her leave, especially considering the way he'd been looking at her. But he didn't know her. They were strangers. So why wouldn't he let her go? There was nothing to keep them together.

She rested and tried to relax, but her concentration broke when she looked up at the tree. The leaves at the top of the tree rustled when the wind blew through them. The branches seemed to dance together with the wind. Her mind brought up a memory, and she remembered that this was the tree under which they had first met. That was when she wanted to touch his hair. That was when he pulled out his knife and aimed it at her. She couldn't help but smile at the thought about it. She had been shocked because no one had ever treated her like that. It had felt rather good in a way. No one in this world knew who she was, so she didn't have to pretend to be someone she was not. Here no one knew who she was, so people didn't have to be nice to her. Of course, these people here had no clue about who she was or where she had come from. And, of course, they wouldn't give her a warm welcome because she was a stranger. She tried to smile, but her smile vanished when she thought about Joey. What was he doing? Was he okay? She felt tears run down her cheeks. She curled up into a ball and cried. The cold air blew, and she shivered. She then remembered that she no longer had her mother's sweater.

She had never wanted to be alone. It would be better traveling with someone else than being alone. She thought about her mother. How must she be feeling? What was she doing right now? Was she at a photo shoot or at home waiting for them? Rena wondered how long she'd been there and how much longer she would have to stay. She remembered her friends and her school. She never thought that she would miss the attention she'd received, but she knew that it wouldn't last very long. It was only her first week of school, and people may have been excited to see her. But later they wouldn't care much. At this new place, people went on with their lives not caring about anything else that went on around them. No one noticed a lonely and lost girl. No one cared to help her or ask her what was wrong. She had known that this day would come. She had known that, one day, it would all go away, but she never thought she would miss her old life. This was what she had wanted all her life—just to be an ordinary girl, but now, since even that was gone, she felt lonely and lost. Why did she feel this way?

She was confused and didn't know what to do. All her life she had taken things for granted. She hadn't been happy and grateful for what she had. She didn't realize that her perfect life was better than anyone could dreamed of. She hadn't cared for what she had. She had wanted things to change, and she hadn't realized that, when they did, she would feel this lonely.

How does Zidika ever survive this life? she wondered. *Like this. How does he go on day after day not talking to anyone? His whole life he has been alone.* "That is not true," she heard Sara speak. "Zidika was not alone his whole life."

"What do you mean? Do you know something?"

"I wasn't going to tell you, but now I think is a better time than ever."

"If you know something, then speak."

"Before, Zidika wasn't always alone. He had me. I was his companion. He was just seventeen when I met him. He was a wandering child when I met him, going from city to city. He was trying to find something. He spoke of a mirror. When I first met him, he couldn't remember anything, not even his own name, but he seemed to have a pretty good memory about where he was from. He talked about it a lot—about strange places I had never heard of. He must have lived far away and somehow got to our place. I agreed to help him search for this mirror. Since he couldn't remember his name, I gave him one. We started out on our journey, but soon he wasn't interested that much about the mirror. He just wanted to be with me and stay by my side. He wanted us to always be together; he didn't want to ever leave him. But our journey grew more dangerous with each passing day. More demons came after us. They were after my power, and I knew I could no longer stay with him. I had to leave him for his own good. I knew he might be angry at me and upset over my leaving. That might be why he's so solitary now. He's so angry that he doesn't let anyone near."

When Sara finished speaking, Rena stayed silent for a while. Then she spoke. "You two must have shared a lot of experiences together."

"Oh, we have," she said in a joyful voice. Even through Rena couldn't see her, she knew what Sara felt. "I have told you everything I wanted you to hear," said Sara. "Now you must decide if you want or need Zidika's help."

Rena sat against the tree and stared at the grass against her feet. She ripped up several stalks and shredded them. She sat with her knees against her chest. Her wounds weren't bothering her. Whatever Zidika had put on them had worked.

"What should I do? I don't want him to get involved with my problems, but I need all the help I can get." At the end of the day she owed him for what he had done. It might have been a small thing, but what Sara had told her about him led her to believe that it must have taken a lot of courage for him to help her, and she was thankful for that. He had gone out of his way to help her and had used his own medicine to heal her wounds, so she shouldn't ask anything from him. She rubbed the side of her stomach, and her finger traced the edge of the bandage. She smiled as it reminded her of him.

She felt her cheeks heating up as she remembered what she had done for him that night. But she couldn't have just left him like that, so she had done what she knew how to do.

Feeling a little tired, she leaned against the tree and closed her eyes for a bit. Exhaustion finally hit her, and she felt herself drifting off to sleep. He was there. She felt his presence nearby; he was coming toward her. He was close, very close. It was as if he was right next to her. Her eyes flew open. She stood up and looked around. But she didn't see him. Maybe she had imagined it all.

How pathetic. She looked back at the tree and then turned around. To her surprise she saw him standing in front of her. Her eyes widened in happiness. All her bad feelings evaporated. She didn't have to think. She knew her decision. Suddenly she felt her body move all on its own. She found herself running forward. All of her fears and worries evaporated as she ran. She just wanted to be in his arms. "Zidika!" she yelled as her arms flew around him. He didn't pull away. Instead, he hugged her back.

Rena was so happy that she started crying, and Zidika felt like a jerk before he realized she was crying because she was happy. She buried her head into the fabric of his jacket. He had made up his mind. He would help her.

CHAPTER 5

Secret Name

. . . .

For the first time in years, Rena felt a sudden change. It was a change that she had wanted for so long, a change that she thought that would never come because she was too afraid of it.

"You must be tired." His voice broke through her thoughts.

Rena stopped walking and stood in front of him until he got a little closer. She turned around and gave him a weak smile and then started walking again. "Will you help me?" She stopped and lowered her voice. She already knew the answer, so why was she asking? The fact that he had followed her all the way said enough, but she wanted to hear it from him.

Zidika got closer to see her face, but she turned away from him. "Help you? You stupid girl, you should already know the answer."

She felt anger when he said that, but at least he had decided to help her. "Who are you calling stupid? For your information, I've been the top student in my class for three years."

"If you tell me your name, I won't have to call you stupid."

Rena fell silent and turned away from Zidika. That's right—she had never told him her name. Well, he hadn't told her his either, but somehow she'd already known his name, so that really didn't count. She thought about all the things that could happen if she told him her name. What if time were changed? What if her future wouldn't be the same anymore? All because she mentioned her name to him. She did not want to mess with time. And besides, what would it do to her? It might make it harder for her to leave. She didn't want that. The thought of leaving already hurt. If she left, then Zidika would be alone, but he was used to being alone. It shouldn't hurt him—or her.

"Why don't you want to tell me?"

"Because I think it's not necessary. When I get what I came here for, I'll leave and you'll never see me again." It stung her when she said those words. And she could tell her words hurt Zidika as well.

"And how can you be so sure we will never see each other again?"

"Believe me, I know. I come from a faraway place."

"So you want me to call you stupid girl the whole time?"

Rena turned around and narrowed her eyes at him. "No," she said angrily.

"Then what do you want me to call you? Halfling?"

Her temper rose, but she did not lose it. The less he knew about her the better. "Daisy." She tried to look at him as seriously as possible.

"You're kidding, right?"

Her eyes darkened. What was up with him? Why couldn't he take a hint and understand that she did not want to tell him? "Yup, that is what I want you to call me from now on."

"Who knows how long we be traveling together? At least until you get what you came here for. And this whole time you want me to call you Daisy?"

Rena turned around and thought to herself that maybe it wasn't such a good idea for him to use that name. It was too much of a weird name anyway. But she couldn't just tell him her name. She had to think of something.

"I know you're joking," Zidika said, sneaking behind her. Panic took over her. Rena turned around, not expecting to see Zidika so close to her. They ended up colliding and falling to the ground. After a few seconds of confusion, Rena realized that she was on top of Zidika.

Zidika's heart was racing so fast. Rena felt her checks heat up. Her heart was pounding so hard against her chest she was sure he could hear it. His amber eyes stared at her, and she could not speak. He looked at her so differently. It made her insides turn. Her heart raced faster, and everything felt still. It was as if there was no one else in the world. Her mind became mush. All her words escaped her as she waited for him to say something. Her heart shook as she heard his quick breathing.

Rena swallowed hard as she waited for him to speak. No one was there except for them. Just the two of them. It felt as if they were the only two people in the world. The shock of his actions almost brought tears to her eyes.

Zidika refused to give up. He flipped Rena over onto her back. "Why won't you tell me?" he spoke in a whisper.

"Zidika, get off," she said with a breathless voice. She felt that, if she told him, her heart would break, and it would be that much harder to leave. She had already planned to leave after the final battle, after she rescued Joey. It was cowardly of her, but Zidika knew she would be leaving. She had told him many times.

"Tell me!" he demanded.

"I can't." She struggled to get up. She picked up her hands and was aiming at him, but he captured both of her hands and pinned them down to the ground. He could see her confusion and the attraction she felt toward him. She just looked so cute when she was angry—when her face turned red and when she looked so hopeless. He knew that this was wrong, but he liked her reactions. He liked bothering her. "Why?" he said.

He was so close that Rena could feel his breath on her skin. "Zidika, get off!" she screamed. To her surprise, she became redder. She tried to fight his … his … charms, but she couldn't give in.

Zidika froze and stared at her. Then he started laughing as he rolled off her. Rena stood up. She crossed her arms and she turned away. "Why do you have to be like this?"

"Why do you have to be like this? Why can't you just tell me your name? Why won't you let me take care of you? Don't you trust me?" He stood up.

"It's not that I don't trust you. I just can't, you see. It's because …" She paused, not finishing her sentence. What was she going to say? That she was from a different time—the future? Then he would definitely look at her weirdly, and maybe he'd decide to not help her. Nothing came to mind. She couldn't think of a good excuse to tell him.

"It's not a hard question," he told her, his eyes darkening. A few minutes passed in silence, and Rena just stood there looking at her feet. Zidika exploded. What was with this girl? Why was she so difficult to deal with? He was trying to help her the best he could. He had just asked her one little thing. Was it so bad to tell him? What was so bad telling someone your name? His fierce amber eyes locked with hers. "So I guess you don't trust me enough to tell me your name." It was driving him crazy. Who was she?

Rena thought that maybe she should tell him. Maybe she had taken this joke of hers a little too far.

"I have to know. I don't think I will be able to help you if you won't tell me." He was going to get some information out of her whether she liked it or not. Rena looked up at him suddenly. She looked so miserable that he was about to let it go and tell her never mind, and just leave the subject. No, he was not going to do that. He was not going to melt an inch. He was not going to let her trick him. Zidika turned away from Rena and slowly started walking away. Why had he ever followed her? What was so wrong telling him her name? She could keep all her other secrets. He just wanted to know her name. This girl was bad news. What other secrets was she hiding? What was the reason for her coming here? To get what?

Helping damsels in distress was something he did not do. He was sure it might come back to bite him in the butt if he chose to stay with her. She needed him. Stupid girl didn't even realize she needed him. He thought that she was different than the others, but she was not. She assessed him just as everybody else did. This girl was bad news if she didn't even want to tell him her name. He was angry at her. It probably sounded ridiculous. She could keep all her secrets. He wouldn't care. Why should he? But he became angrier by the second. Not knowing her name made him angry, and the conflict was tiring him. He wanted to shout out in anger. Why? He didn't know. He just wanted her name, that's all. He should just leave her and never look back, never see those beautiful eyes or hear her voice. If she wasn't going to tell him, he didn't need to know. He was going to leave her right now.

The forest was silent. He didn't hear anyone or anything. He rather hoped that the girl would follow him. She didn't. He thought about their little argument just now and it made him feel a bit better. He wanted to turn back and go to her, but he wasn't going to do that. If she wanted his help, if she so needed his help, as she had she told him, then she would have to come out and tell him her name if she wanted him back. He didn't turn around to check.

"Rena, why are you being so stubborn?" Sara asked.

"I'm not you," Rena answered. "Anybody should know that my being here could mess up time."

Could mess up time? She sounded as if she was going to laugh.

"Rena, time will not get messed up. You were supposed to come here for a reason. You were sent here. I may not know that reason, but I can say that you shouldn't be afraid to tell him your name."

"Really?" Rena spoke with joy in her voice. She quickly started running after Zidika.

A branch broke behind him. Zidika quickly turned around. He saw Rena looking at him with tearstained eyes. She was so happy she was able to tell him her name that she couldn't keep the tears back. She blinked them away as she looked up at him. "Rena. My name is Rena." It sounded like music to his ears. It was a nice name.

CHAPTER 6

Trapped

· · · · · · · ·

I t felt good telling him her name. She felt relived, as if she was telling him all her problems. Rena knew that she must not waste any time and that she should get going as soon as possible. Even though she was here, she felt as if she was trapped. She knew what she had to do, but she didn't know where to begin. She didn't know where to go. What should she do? When she did find her brother, what next? How would she free him? How would she defeat the centipede? But the big questions remained and stayed glued in her head: What if she couldn't defeat the centipede? What if she couldn't bring her brother home with her? What if …

"Rena." Zidika looked at her with a worried look. Rena returned her attention back to reality.

She looked terrified as she stared out into space. "Are you okay?" he asked, looking more worried.

Rena forced a smile. "Yeah, I'm all right. Just thinking about something. No need to worry." But deep inside he knew she wasn't okay, and it worried him. He knew she was freaking out about all that was happening.

She couldn't get the questions out of her head. Voices of dear friends and other people circled her head like an unstopping game. They asked her many questions. What should she do? What if it doesn't work? What if she wouldn't be able to find Joey? What if she didn't get to return home?

What would she do then? Their questions in her head were relentless. "Stop it!" she yelled, and then she no longer heard the voices.

Zidika looked her, more worried than ever, and this time he wasn't going to take her "I'm okay" speech. "Rena, what's bothering you?" he asked in a gentle voice. He was going to protect her. Whatever her problem was, he was going to help her solve it. He would catch her and always protect her. Even if saving her killed him, he would protect her.

"Nothing's bothering me really." She looked up at him, and this time she did not smile. She had that sad look.

"Don't give me that! For crying out loud, you just screamed at something. I want to know what's bothering you."

"Like I said already, it's none of your concern. It's my business, and I need to deal with it alone." She walked right past him.

Zidika looked at her. Deal with it alone? Didn't she realize he would be helping her? They would be on a journey together. She should tell him what was bothering her. This girl was strange in many more ways than one.

Entering the house, Rena realized that her arm was bleeding and that she was wearing her bloody and smelly clothes. She tried to relive the pain by rubbing her hand on the wound, but that only made it bleed more. "Let me see that," Zidika demanded. He held her arm and studied the wound. He did not let go of her hand while he reached for a box of bandages. He gently took care of her wound.

Rena rubbed her arm as he let go of it. "Can you be a little gentler?" She walked to the window and sat down on the bed.

"Rena," he said, leaning against the wooden counter.

Rena looked up at him. "Yes?"

He walked up to her. "You're not alone, so don't act like you are." Then he walked back to the counter.

Rena looked out the window and found herself saying, "Sara and you are really close." She turned around to see his reaction.

"How do you know her?" he asked as he put away the bandages. Zidika did not show much emotion.

"Well, you could say that we are really close."

Zidika turned around and looked straight at Rena. Oh maybe she shouldn't have said that. "How close?" He studied her, waiting for her reaction, her answer.

She felt that, if she made the slightest move or made a mistake, he would get angry. His eyes blazed. This was a side of him that Rena hadn't seen yet. "Closer than you know." Rena whispered, making sure that he did not hear her.

Zidika stood in the same spot, not moving, staring at her as if he was trying to make her confess by staring her down. "I'm waiting."

"Why does it matter to you? What if I don't want to say?" She smirked, finding herself acting like a little kid.

"I just wanted to know the history you have with her that's all." But his eyes stared coldly back at her as if she had said or done something wrong. His hands where forming into fists, and he seemed angry.

"My history with Sara? I can't really tell you much about her. It seems we have sort of known each other but never really talked till recently." Rena noticed his eyes widen. His gaze shot at her like daggers. He looked as if he was going to hurt someone. "Why are you telling me this? Why are you doing this? Did someone send you here to torment me?"

Oh, no! Now she had pushed his buttons. She shouldn't have said anything or even mentioned Sara at all. How stupid of her to say something like that now. "Zidika, what are you saying? I don't know what you mean." Rena found herself biting her lip in concern.

He came closer to Rena, his eyes cold and his hands clinched into fists. "Sara vanished a year ago without a trace. Poof! She was gone. No one has seen her since then, and you're telling me that you talked to her!"

"Zidika, it's a bit difficult to explain. You see, my history with Sara is different than what you would think." What was wrong with him? Why wouldn't he even listen?

"Lies! Why are you lying to me?" he yelled.

"Zidika, calm down." Rena got up and changed her tone. Then Rena understood that Sara was speaking. She walked up to Zidika. "Get ahold of yourself," she said with seething eyes. She looked disappointed at him. "Why are you being like this? Tell me. Let it all out," she said, her voice a little calming.

As if he understood that something had changed about Rena, Zidika seemed to calm down a little. He looked at Rena and then sat down on a chair. He looked at her with eyes that seemed to be crying. Rena did not like the way he looked. She didn't want to see him upset. Before then he had looked even scarier, and Rena had never seen that side of him. It scared her, and she never wanted to see him like that.

"I'm sorry, Rena. It's just that sometimes I get upset when someone mentions her name. And when you said that you had talked to her just recently, I just totally exploded." Then he changed the subject. "You were kidding when you said that you had talked to her, right?" He tried to sound sarcastic, but there was doubt his voice as well.

Rena looked away. "About that …" She tried not to speak loud enough for him to hear her, but he spoke before she could even begin her sentence.

"I don't know how you could know her. Maybe someone told you about her. She is pretty famous here for what she did for a lot of people. Everyone knew and loved her. She was a hero to a lot of people."

"What did she do?"

"She solved people's problems. If they needed a demon slain, she would do it. If they needed her to purify a certain thing, she would do it. If someone needed a priestess, she would take that part. She was an amazing woman." He spoke about her with a blissful look. He was transformed into a totally different person. One minute he was shooting daggers at her with his eyes; the next he was talking about a girl so happily, as if he liked her. For some reason, it made Rena … jealous.

"How did you guys meet?" She found herself asking the question even though she knew the whole story.

His eyes twinkled. "It didn't happen long ago, maybe a year. I met her by accident while I was looking for something had I lost."

"By any chance was it a mirror?"

Zidika looked at her with a serious look. "How would you know?"

"I used a mirror to travel here," she whispered, not thinking that Zidika would hear her.

Zidika got up from his seat and looked at her, his eyes so serious. "What did you say? How did you know about that? Is it true—what you just said?"

Rena did not look at him in the eye. She looked away. She hadn't thought that he would actually hear her. "Nothing. I was talking to myself. Anyway, why would you care?" Zidika sat back down. "If I told you, you wouldn't believe me."

"I've seen a lot of things that I thought I would never see."

"Well," said Zidika, "you are right about that. This is a very different place. Here we can let our inner powers come out. Sometimes they are powers we thought we never had. The inner powers of every human who travels to this place come out when they are most in need. This land is the only spiritual place in the world."

"So what you're saying," said Rena, "is that we all have powers, but they come out only when we are in a magical and spiritual place like this? You're saying that something like this may never happen in the real world?

"What are talking about—the real world? This is the real world."

"I mean … I was talking to myself again." She had almost forgotten that this was not the place she knew.

"Anyway," Zidika said, "you were telling me about Sara. You talked to me about her as if she is still here."

"Because she is here." Rena paused. Could he know that Sara was inside of her? "As long as we keep thinking about this person, and keep her in our hearts, this will always be the place she belongs. It will be her home." He looked at Rena. His eyes were different, and Rena felt as if she could stare into his eyes forever without looking away. But Rena felt, inside of her, that she needed to say this no matter what it was. Maybe she should tell him that Sara was inside of her. She opened her mouth to speak, but the boy spoke first.

"You know I'm not helping you because you are …" He paused. "It's because I feel that helping you is what she would have wanted me to do. You seem different from other people. You are different in a good way." Rena felt as if that was a lie. It was as if he had slightly forced the words. "Besides," he continued, "it would be nice to leave this little house and go on an adventure. Only this time it will be with you." He stared at Rena.

Rena blushed, and no matter what she thought of, it wouldn't change. She turned away so he wouldn't see her.

"Hey, Rena, can I ask you something?" It was Sara.

Rena rolled her eyes, annoyed. "What is it?"

"Can I use your body?" Rena gasped. Why on earth would she ask that? Why would she want to? She should already know the answer! This was her body, and Sara was already using it without her permission, so how dare she ask to use her body?

"No! Of course not! What are you thinking?"

"I just want him to see me—the real me."

"Well, still the answer is no," Rena whispered, and this time she made sure that he could not hear her.

Suddenly a shockwave hit her. She felt as if she was being possessed by something. She couldn't move. She felt as if something was taking control of her body. It was as if she was being locked out of her body. She felt her hair changing color. She immediately knew what was going on.

CHAPTER 7

Sara

• • • • • •

"Zidika, don't you remember me?" Sara stood up.

Zidika looked at her, not realizing what had just happened, not realizing who was standing in front of him. What was going on here? What just happened? Who was standing in front of him? Was it still Rena? "How did you do that?" he said staring at Rena in amazement. Then he realized who was standing right before his eyes. "Sara." He had hardly recognized her. He couldn't explain the joy he felt when he saw her. It was like a miracle to finally see her again. She hadn't changed; in fact, she looked very much like Rena. His smile widened, and he got up and walked close to her.

"It's been a long time since I saw you," she said smiling back at him. "You were seventeen."

"And I still am. Not much time has passed since you disappeared."

"Actually, a lot of time has passed." She said it in a whisper. But Zidika changed the topic.

"Why did you leave me, Sara? I missed you so much," he said, coming closer to her.

Sara backed away a little. "Zidika, aren't you angry at me for leaving? For not telling you? For breaking my promise to you?"

"Why should I be angry at you when you have done so much for me?" he said in a sweet voice, coming still closer.

"I left you without telling you, and you're not angry? But when Rena mentioned my name, you seemed to want to hurt the poor girl." She closed her eyes so she would not be tempted to shout as Zidika had done.

Then his eyes grew a little cold. He looked down at his hands. "Then why? Tell me why you left. Tell me why you didn't tell me and why you left me all by myself. You knew that I was still adjusting to my power. You knew that demons would be after me. You knew all that and still left." He looked back at her, disappointed. He looked heartbroken.

"Zidika, if you would just listen to me." She tried to tell him something, but Zidika was too stubborn to listen.

"Why? Just tell me why. If it was for my own good, then I don't want to hear it."

Sara looked down, disappointed in herself. She tried to think of a way to tell him, but every idea she had felt meaningless. "If demons were after your power and my life was getting more dangerous by the day, I wouldn't care. I wouldn't care if I was in danger. All I wanted to do was be with you." Sara kept all her emotions sealed up inside of her. She only half formed her words as she tried to tell him. There was no excuse—no reason—for what she had done to him. She had hurt him badly without realizing it. And only now did she understand, now when she was only a reflection of the real person, an illusion. Her real body is gone, and she had stayed in one host for a long time. "There is no excuse for what I have done to you. I understand that now. I thought I was doing the right thing by leaving you, by not telling you so you wouldn't follow me. But I was only hurting myself. I didn't realize I had caused you so much pain, emotional and physical."

Zidika looked at her as if he had been waiting for her to say those words. "How was it that you were able to do that? Where is your real body?"

"I hid it where no one would find it. Most of the power is within my body, but I have a portion of it with me. That is how I was able to change. That's how the demon found me."

"So, you have been living inside this girl's body to prevent the demons from finding you?"

"Yes. So much time has passed that I wasn't able to disappear from this world. I may no longer have my body, but I still have my soul, for I am not able to disappear from this world."

"Sara, you always talked like this, and I was never able to understand you. For example, you said many years have passed. It's been only a … well, it's been almost a year."

"Zidika, what we are doing is wrong. We shouldn't be doing this. Simply put, it's not really me. I'm using Rena's body."

But it was as if her words never got through to him. He didn't seem to mind. He came close to her. "So what? You can control her. You can have her body."

Rena forced herself back, not believing he had said something so selfish. Was this the Zidika she thought he was, or was this the real Zidika? Still, it hurt that he had said that. She was angry and upset that dear Sara had done this to her. Now dear Zidika had suggested that awful idea to Sara. How dare they! Rena wanted to scream. She wanted her body back, but she knew that she didn't have the power to take it.

"Zidika, I can't do that." Sara could feel Rena's emotions, and she understood how she felt. Sara just wanted to make this simple and quick without hurting anyone. She spoke in a sweet voice.

"You're like a little brother to me, and I know you look up to me as your older sister, but I cannot use this girl's body. You see, I brought her into this mess, and I'm going to fix it. That's what you must understand."

"But I don't understand. You're more to me than an older sister! You're like a mother! You are my whole family! He looked down and then straight up again as he asked Sara the same question again: "Why did you have to leave me? I don't get it. Why did you just vanish all of a sudden?"

"I did it for you," she said as tears reflected her emotions. "I didn't want you to get hurt. You mean so much to me. I didn't want you to get mixed up with my problems."

"Will you hurt me again? You said you were protecting me, but you were the one actually running away."

"Zidika, you've got to understand me. Many demons are after my power, and because of me, an innocent boy got involved. He had nothing do with this, and yet a demon possessed him. I must help Rena find him. It's the least I can do."

Zidika looked at her with flaming eyes. "I don't want to hear your excuses." He spoke in a loud voice. He looked as if he didn't want to listen to anybody. He thought of Sara as more than a mother. He loved her. And then, all at once, it hit him like an exploding bomb. He thought he had locked away his feelings when Sara left. But this girl suddenly showed up with the key to emotions he thought he would never have again. And now he learned that she had his old love inside of her. It was one big jumble of mess. It was too much news for him to handle all at once.

Sara gently slapped Zidika. She gave him a look he had never seen before. "Stop this! Get ahold of yourself. I know what I did was wrong, and I'm willing to pay for it. But what you're doing is far worse than what I did. I'm here to help people, not destroy their lives. You've got to understand that. Didn't you learn anything when we were together?" Her tone changed, and Zidika saw tears. "I missed you so much."

He finally broke, and all the emotions that where inside escaped. He hugged Sara. "I don't ever want to let you go. Now that your back, I'm not letting go of you ever again."

Sara looked at him with tears in her eyes. "Zidika, I don't ever want to leave you again, but you said it yourself. As long as we think about a person, there is always a home for him or her to return to."

"Those where just words that meant nothing."

"Those weren't just empty words. They meant something. They made me so happy." She smiled.

But Zidika didn't want to understand. "I don't want you to go. I'm not going to let you."

"Do you remember my promise to you?" she asked. "Since I won't be here, I pass that promise along to Rena. She will help you find the mirror. I'm sure of it. Zidika, please. This doesn't have to be like this."

Wait, thought Rena. *When does Sara have the right to make decisions for me? I haven't agreed to anything. In fact, I'm against all of this! This jerk may have been hurt. I understand that. But he doesn't have to take it out on me! I haven't done anything to him. I'm not involved in this mess.*

Zidika was talking to Sara again. "So what? She's just a girl. You're the person I really want. You have been like a mother, like family. That's something I never got to experience until I met you, when I finally understood what it's like to care for someone. What it's like to be happy and loved. So, keep her body and let's travel together like the old times."

Sara protested. "And lock her up in her own body? She wouldn't have anywhere to go. At least I have the black pearl. She will die if we keep her isolated. She will have nowhere to go."

Rena didn't want to hear any more of this. She yelled inside her head and fought as best she could. "Enough!" Rena shouted inside. "Enough!" She shouted even louder, noticing that she had her own body back. Her hair changed back into her original color. Zidika was still hugging her. When he realized it wasn't his beloved Sara, he let go of her as if he had been stung, and he backed away from her suddenly as if he was afraid of what Rena's reaction might be. He couldn't even look at her. He muttered something she couldn't hear and headed for the door. He tried to ignore the guilt in his gut. After he left, Rena listened until she couldn't hear his footsteps anymore.

Rena fell down on her knees, not believing that Sara could do that. She felt so helpless, so useless. She had no one. No one. She was all alone. Why hadn't she been able to stop Sara from taking control of her body? Sara just had much more power than she did. She noticed a stream of tears on her cheeks and remembered that Sara had been crying, but then she realized they were her own tears. She wiped the moisture from on her checks.

Rena was so hurt and so upset that she just wanted to escape her situation for a minute. She wished she had never had followed her brother. But she couldn't let her emotions cloud her judgement, and she realized what she thought was wrong. But most of all, she hated herself. She hated that she was weak, and she wished that she could be that carefree person she once had been—that strong girl who loved every part of her life, that girl whose eyes could glow with excitement. She still was that person, but she had changed. She had grown up enough to understand that she couldn't take this treatment anymore—all this attention … attention for no reason. She had stopped caring about everything else and had locked herself away from the world. Sometimes the old her would shine back in, and she would be that joyful and outgoing person, but as soon as she discovered what had happened, she would lock herself back up. Why did she care so much about this? She should just get over it the way she dealt with other things. But something about her situation just stung her in the place it hurt most—her heart.

"I just wish I was that kind of person," she told herself. "That blissful person." She couldn't remember the reason she had become so isolated from the world. Then an image sprang into her head and played out like a movie. She watched what had happened three years ago. She became silent as her eyes widened in sadness. She smiled bitterly and covered her face with her hands. She had been only eleven then, but she had been old enough to realize what she had done, and she blamed herself for it. Even through everyone clearly saw that it wasn't her fault, she couldn't help but beat herself up for it.

***

When Zidika came back, he didn't look at her or speak for the rest of the day. He didn't even look in her direction. He was angry, and so was she. They were silent for the rest of the day, but it was killing both of them. Neither of them could take the silence. Rena was angry for what he wanted to do. She was miserable. She understood what misery felt like, but this wasn't the kind she had felt before. This was different. She wanted him gone. She wanted him to disappear from her life. But then she returned from her world of despair and faced the world of reality she had to face. There was nothing to do. She had to face Zidika. The voice in her head told her she couldn't get rid of Sara no matter what she tried. Sara was a part of her. She wished this all had never happened. She wished this world would disappear. She wished she had never met him. She wished her life would go back to normal. She wanted to be a normal girl again living her ordinary life that didn't involve magic. Yes, as much as she hated to say it, she missed her old life. She wanted to go back to school and forget about all of this. She wanted to eat cake after school with everyone and enjoy their company. She wanted to watch her mother's modeling shoot and also be in it. She wanted to meet with her friends after school and just have fun going to the park or working on school assignments. She did not want to have to find her brother out there in that different, magical, dangerous world that she had no clue about. When she finally found her brother, what would they do then? How would she convince her brother to go back with her? How would she free him from the centipede? Why did she need Zidika? She could do this alone without him, right? But the truth was that she just couldn't. She had to admit that she needed his help. He knew this place better than she did, and it hurt to admit that she needed him. She had no one except for him, a boy who was so different now from the way she thought he was when she first met him.

Everything was silent around the house. Rena felt very lonely. She felt like that hopeless little girl again, the one who needed help. She was going to burst into tears, and she needed someone. She felt cold all around her. She felt emotionally cold. It was as if the atmosphere around her felt her pain.

Rena lay down silently and looked up at the ceiling, imagining bright tiny stars up there staring right back at her feeling her pain and misery. She wanted someone; she needed someone. She couldn't imagine why she had let this get her down. Why did she feel protective? Why did it matter what he thought about? She was thinking about him too much. It was stressful. She curled herself into a ball under her covers and slowly closed her eyes.

"Daddy!" A girl who looked to be the age of seven was hugging her teddy bear tightly. "But, Papa, you promised!" She spoke in a sweet, childish voice. She wore her hair in two pigtails, each tied with a bunny hair tie. A tall man with sweet, gentle brown eyes knelt in front of Rena. "My sweet girl, I promise you, after work," he said, hugging little Rena. Rena smiled as she recalled the memory. Then the last thing she could remember as she drifted off to sleep was her father's soft and melodic voice.

CHAPTER 8

The River

. . . .

Rena awoke as her dream became a nightmare in which she was forced to recall that horrible day three years earlier. She remembered everything that had happened. Raising her head from her pillow, she looked around for Zidika, but he was nowhere in sight. Thinking he might have left, she went over to the drawer and fished out some clean clothes. They were boyish clothes, and they looked bigger than her usual size. She had obviously grabbed the first thing she could reach. But she didn't want to put the clothes on. She still smelled like blood, and she thought that a bath would take away the terrible stench.

She looked outside the window and saw the moon's blue light shining through the trees. And nearby, beyond the trees, she saw a waterfall. She smiled and walked outside. She wanted to get rid of all her horrible memories—to forget for at least a second, and not to feel the pain in her chest as she remembered everything that had happened. She never wanted to remember again. This day was turning out to be horrible.

A cool breeze blew and twirled all around her. Her hair danced in the wind. As she looked up at the sky, she saw a clear, bright light. It was the most amazing and magical thing she had ever seen. Beautiful shades of blue, pink, and purple painted the sky, glittering ever so beautifully. Rena never imagined that she would see something as breathtaking. Yet she quickly wanted to go to the river and take a dip in the cooling water.

When she reached the waterfall, Rena set the clean clothes down on a rock and took off her favorite blue tank top and black jeans. Getting into the water, Rena could already feel it soothing her, rippling through her fingers as it cleared her body and soul. She felt the water's refreshment as it cleared her thoughts and washed the terrible memories from deep inside of her and pushed the thoughts back into her mind. It felt good not having to worry about anything else in the world, not having a care in the world. She felt her body calm down as she leaned herself back into the falling water. Laughing out loud, Rena got up and closed her eyes. She scooped up handfuls of water and splashed it everywhere, all around her. She felt so relieved, so alive. The waterfall surely made her feel at peace with herself. She no longer had to fight with herself, blame herself. Rena stood under the waterfall and allowed the cool water to run down freely on her body. She closed her eyes and just listened to the sound of the water as it slowly took hold of her. As her hair fell over her shoulders and covered her face, she rested her head on a rock.

***

Zidika had just returned from his walk. This was his usual time—when it was dark and the moon shone its light where he went, creating a path for him to walk on. This was the time when he would spend time outdoors looking up at the sky as it revealed its magic. He looked at the bright moon as it revealed the waterfall and a girl sleeping on a rock next to the roaring water. Her long blond hair covered her face and chest. She looked so peaceful as she slept by the waterfall. Her wet hair sparkled in the moonlight. Mystified by this girl, Zidika had to retreat and continue his journey home. He walked a few feet forward, but then stopped and looked back. The trees had covered the waterfall, and the moon no longer shone down on it.

He walked into the house not realizing that Rena was gone. Walking over to a drawer, he took out another blanket and placed it on the floor. He tried to find a place for himself to sleep. He didn't want to be next to Rena. She still hadn't talked to him yet. If she wasn't going to say something, why should he be the first to speak?

When Zidika finally realized what was going on—what he'd said to Sara—he wished he hadn't. Not only had he upset Rena, but he had upset Sara too, and she was the last person he wanted to see upset. He felt bad about what he had said. No, he felt horrible, and he wished he could somehow make it up to her.

***

The roaring sound of the water behind her reminded Rena of the roaring sound of her father's truck. Now she was forced to remember, to relive the moments. Rena jolted awake, not realizing she had fallen asleep. The pain in Rena's chest was so unbearable that it felt as if everything was more real than ever. She wiped the sweat off her forehead. She wanted her muscles and nerves to calm down. Her past was haunting her more than ever now, and she felt the need to escape.

She approached the rock where she had left the clean clothes and slowly dressed herself. She picked up her old clothes and slowly walked toward the house, bitterly remembering what Zidika had wanted to do. When she arrived at the door, she slowly stepped inside, trying not to awaken the sleeping Zidika. But her attempts were in vain. Before she could put her clothes away, Zidika lit a candle. "So you're the mystery thief," he said, staring awkwardly at Rena. She looked at him with a dangerous scowl on her face. She quickly turned away and settled her clothes on the chair next to her. "Where were you?" he asked his town changing.

"And why should I tell you? It's my own life, and I can live it how I want to. I don't need someone controlling my every move," she bitterly said, her face darkening, making Zidika feel even more horrible and a bigger jerk.

"Rena," he said in an apologetic tone.

"I don't want to hear it."

"Let me explain."

"Explain what!" She turned around felling angry and a bit jealous. Her temper rose, and she felt as if she couldn't control herself. "What you said really hurt me." She shot him an ugly and dangerous look.

With that he could not argue. "I get what you're saying but—"

"Am I really so unimportant to you that you would rather have someone who isn't a part of this life anymore? Someone who's practically dead? You would sell me out for a past life? A memory?" She was seething in anger.

For some reason, that did not bother Zidika. All he cared about now was getting things strait with Rena. "Listen, Rena—"

She shook her head. "What is there to listen to? You said enough to Sara." She looked at him ever more dangerously. Then her gaze fell to the floor, and she saw a blanket almost next to hers. She growled. "What is this?" she pointed.

Zidika looked at the two blankets almost next to each other.

Her eyes shot up in anger. She wanted to shout out on the top of her lungs. Zidika tried to explain, which he immediately regretted when he saw the look she gave him. It was a dirty look. She let a string of curses out under her breath and stormed out of the house. He stood still listening as she closed the door behind her and quickened her pace a run. Zidika did not bother to look back or follow her. He knew the answer already. It was all his fault.

As she walked along the moonlit path, her hair tangled in the wind and she watched the starlit sky. She was angry, but mostly she wanted to cry.

CHAPTER 9

Kori Shimo

• • • • • • • • • • • • •

When she had calmed herself and relaxed, Rena sat next to the waterfall and listened to the water crashing down against the rocks. The sound relaxed her. She felt better. She touched the water and soon noticed it was freezing her hand. The water had suddenly changed. It had been warm, and now it was freezing cold, and it wasn't that cold outside. It was as if the water felt her pain and reflected her heart, as if she herself had turned the water ice cold.

She glared at her refection in the water. Her eyes locked onto the person she was staring at. A tear escaped her eye and trailed down her cheek, finally making its way to the water, mixing in with the bright blue, moonlit ripples. She dipped her hand in once more, fanning it back and forth. The ripples shattered her refection.

All of a sudden, the water started turning into ice. As Rena watched it happen, she could hardly believe it. Was this all her? Was she doing this? She stood up as the waterfall turned completely into ice. "What is happening?" she asked, dumbstruck as she stood shocked in her spot. She touched the water again, and the ice started slowly melting away. "What is happening?" she asked again a little scared.

"Oh, look we have a kori shimo." Sara spoke.

Rena's blood boiled as she heard her voice. Sara wasn't completely to blame for what Zidika had said. Still, Rena didn't want to talk to her right now.

"If you're wondering what a kori shimo—"

"Sara, I don't want to talk to you."

"Why not? Are you still mad about what happened?"

"Sara, just leave me alone. I have to spend my whole life with you, so just leave me alone this once."

"But don't you want to find out what you did right now?"

"That was me?"

"Do you see anyone else here?"

"But how did I do that?"

"We call people like you kori shimo. They are people who can turn anything they touch into freezing cold water or snow. When you're really angry, you can even cause a blizzard. Your actions reflect your heart and what you are feeling at the time. I guess the pain you felt caused the water to freeze."

Rena felt a bit angry when she heard the last sentence. "It's amazing a blizzard didn't occur, considering how angry I was."

"Yes, it happens when you're upset or angry."

"Why do I have it?"

"You're not the only one who has it. A lot of people like you have this power, and they're not aware of it."

"But what does this have to do with me? I'm not even from this world."

"It can happen to anyone. Everyone has this special power of their own, they just don't know about it. It doesn't happen in your world because you have no magic, but in this world … well, a lot of things can happen." She spoke in a different, softer tone. "Actually only woman have this kind of power—to turn anything we touch to ice. And there are many more other kinds of powers that people aren't aware of. People don't know that they have these powers within them. They live their lives as ordinary humans. But when something like this does occur, they don't know how to deal with it and often run away from their villages thinking they have been cursed."

"That's kinda cool, but scary at the same time. What other powers are there?"

"Kari kaias are fire breathers. Kasumi kamas can bend water to their will. We woman possess those kinds of powers. It is said that guys don't really possess the kind of power we woman do, but if they did, it would be the rarest of them all. I heard it is then called ckii tsuki, and the power actually turns the moon red. It is an extremely powerful power. I have never come across anyone with this particular power, but I have always wanted to meet one."

"Those poor people living their lives in fear because of their own powers," said Rena. "I wish I could help them."

"You can!"

"What?"

"I do not know how you would do it, but I'm sure you could be successful. You're a strong and beautiful girl. You can do anything if you put your mind to it."

"But I don't have time to save other people. I can't even save my own brother." Rena smiled. This little chat with Sara had made her feel better, and discovering her new power excited her. She marched back to the house. She barged in leaving the door open, so the moonlight shone in.

Zidika sat on the chair next to her blanket. He picked up her old clothes and handed them to Rena. "I took the time to wash them for you. You'd better be thankful."

Rena forced a smile instead of shouting at him, hiding the fact that she was still mad at him. "We are leaving, so pack your bags," she said in a cold tone.

"What do you mean we are leaving? It's the middle of the night."

"Well, I can't wait any longer. You at least owe me that much because of what you did."

"What are you talking about? I have done enough for you already. In the morning, we leave. Right now, get some sleep." His tone had changed as his blood had turned cold.

"What do you mean?"

They continued their useless banter until Sara broke out in Rena's head. "Quiet!" she shouted so loud Rena's head started spinning. "Rena, you can't leave right now. You've had barely a wink of sleep. Go to bed, and you'll get a bright start tomorrow."

Rena frowned sadly as those words reminded her of her mother. She used to speak like that—in that very same tone—whenever Rena wouldn't listen or she wanted Rena to do something. Rena's eyes widened, and tears sprang into them. "Mother," she quietly said. Then she remembered everybody at home, and she knew that she missed them. Rena allowed her tears to run down along with her thoughts as she tried to put the pieces together. Everything combined—her thoughts, her emotions, and what she had felt all along. She felt like breaking down, like a little girl in her mother's arms. She looked at the floor. "Who will find Joey? Who will rescue him? Who will bring him back home?" Her eyes teared up. Her emotions were bringing her back to her real problem and why she had come there in the first place. "Fine," she said. She lay down and wrapped herself in the blanket, letting the warmth calm her and make her sleepy. Rena remained motionless, her hands flat out beside her. She remembered all the good times she'd had with her brother, which caused her to break down. She knew she was going to cry, and she wanted somebody to console her.

CHAPTER 10

A Day at the Beach

· ·

The next day, Rena dragged Zidika to one village after the other. By the end of the day, they were exhausted. They had gathered no information. Rena did not know what to ask about. She did not know the name of the demon that had possessed Joey. She did not know what it looked like other than that it was a huge centipede. Zidika and Rena both sat against a tree staring at each other.

"What was the reason for this?" Zidika asked.

"I already told you—to get information about the centipede."

"This boy who has been possessed by the centipede, does he mean a lot to you?"

Rena looked down at her hands. She didn't want to tell him. She didn't want to reveal too much information about her family, and she definitely didn't want to show her emotions. She looked back up at him. "Yes, he's my brother. I grew up with him. We are more than your average brother and sister. We were friends—best friends. We were always there for each other, no matter what."

"Seems he means a lot to you."

"He does, and I'm not leaving without him." She kicked at the ground in anger. "And the only information I have is that he is somewhere where a lot of dangerous demons live."

"Where is it?"

"I don't know. A girl told me that it is across the ocean on that island." She pointed to a small, rounded half circle of an island that was visible across the ocean.

"Are you planning to go there?"

"Well, I have to check everyplace he might be!"

"I think we are too exhausted to go anywhere today. Let's get some rest and get an early start tomorrow."

Both Zidika and Rena walked to the beach. Rena sat down and stared at the ocean while Zidika went to get some firewood, since they would be camping for the night. Rena loved the beach. She loved just sitting on the sand and staring out into the ocean, watching as the waves crashed against each other and the shore. Zidika had no complaints about the beach either. The beach was a calming place to be.

Suddenly, Zidika heard yelling. He quickly rushed back to Rena with all his strength and all his might. He found Rena stomping her foot at something in the sand. "What's going on?"

"This stupid crab pinched me and then ran away down into its hole!" Zidika tried his best not to laugh at this girl who was different and not like most girls who were afraid of tiny crabs. Zidika dropped the wood that he had gathered and walked over to Rena. She turned around, her hands flying in the air, and she almost hit him. "Hey, let's go for a swim," she said suddenly and smiled. Rena turned around and ran straight for the shallow water. She twisted and turned as if dancing with no music. The warm water felt nice, and she didn't have to worry about anything else, at least for a bit. The warm sand underneath her toes felt nice—until she tripped and fell splashing into the water. She laughed and looked at Zidika, who stood at the edge of the ocean with his feet in the water.

Zidika thought she looked cute—extremely cute—when she was so happy. She smiled brightly at him and waved at him, inviting him to get into the water. But when he still stood in the same spot, Rena scooped up at handful of water and threw it at him. His eyes grew wide. He ran into the water and passed Rena. She was surprised when he picked her up from behind and held her above him. Rena screamed as he dropped her into the water. She quickly stood up, scooped up a bunch of water, and threw it at him.

Zidika looked at her, irritated. Why was she acting like this? Hadn't she been furious at him the other day? Had she forgotten about that? It didn't bother him. At least she wasn't targeting him now. She giggled and threw more water at him. She had acted so coldly to him the other day. Now she was playing in the water and making him join in as well. It took him by surprise, but he liked seeing Rena so happy. She was letting her emotions out. She wasn't the angry girl she'd been before.

"What is this? Quit messing around!" he warned her. Either she didn't hear a word he'd said, or she chose to ignore him. She splashed more water at him and ran away. Zidika looked at her in a strange way. What was she doing? This was no time to be messing around. Had she gone crazy? Or was this a game? He hoped it was a game.

Rena stopped running and looked back at Zidika. Just then a large wave came toward her. It drenched her and caused her to fall on her back. She screamed as she fell. When she got up, she started laughing and had a stupid expression on her face. "Zidika!" she yelled, pushing her hair back.

He narrowed his eyes and then jumped forward, sending another wave toward her. Rena escaped the wave and also jumped forward sending a mini wave to completely soak Zidika. "Rena!" he yelled. He stood up and ran after her. Rena ran a few feet away from Zidika. She looked back to see that he was quite far away from her. She watched as Zidika made another wave and forced it at her. One wave came at her, and then another and another. Rena backed away a few feet, not watching where she was going. She tried to get herself away from the wall of water. As the waves lunged at her, Rena giggled one last time before she fell into a hole. She tried to get up, but her feet didn't touch the sand. With all that water splashing at her, it was hard to keep her balance and not go underwater. She spit out salt water in disgust as she tried to breathe.

Zidika kept forming more waves that kept coming toward her. She was too far off, so Zidika couldn't see her getting washed away. He was going to win this game. He wondered how she would get him after this. A hand flew up out of the water, and soon Zidika stopped making waves. The hand vanished, and so did Rena. He didn't want her to get hurt. Where was she? She was gone.

***

Rena woke up coughing up a large quantity of water. She gasped for air as she lay on the cold floor. Breathing heavily, she managed to use her arms to pull herself up. Her body ached all over as she stood up. Her arms and legs felt like lead. A coldness surrounded her, and she didn't know where she was. Her first concern was how she had got there. She wondered if Zidika had noticed that she was gone. Rena looked up. A faint light shone through the ceiling. It shone down onto a tiny waterfall that ran down small rocks and into a small pool of water. As the water ran down into the pool, it sounded pleasant and peaceful. A layer of sand scrunched beneath her feet. Where was she? She knew she was in a cave, but where was the cave? Was it underwater? Had she entered by an underwater route when she fell into the hole?

In the back of her mind she was more worried when she wondered if Zidika noticed that she was gone. Was he happier without her? Did he feel happy that he had finally got rid of her? She tried not to let that thought depress her. Maybe she was worrying for nothing. Maybe those worries were all in her head. She felt dizzy thinking about this. She shouldn't worry so much.

She looked up at the huge rock. She had to get out of there. She couldn't waste any time there. How was Zidika going to find her now? She closed her eyes and searched deep inside herself. She had been in a similar situation before when she was traveling though the mirror. But she couldn't use the sword to help her this time.

She used her feet and arms to pick herself up and begin to climb the rock. Her arms hurt as she put more weight on them, but she had to keep going. She was terrified and hadn't even imagined that she had the strength to do this. She realized that people never know what they might be able to do until they had to do it! This was her; this was definitely the old Rena.

Do not look down! she told herself as she kept climbing. Her feet and hands were scratched up and hurt like crazy, but she was almost there, almost to the small faint light she saw before her. Her hands held the ledge so tightly while she walked to the next place that looked climbable. If she made any mistake, she would fall to her death, and then what would happen to Joey and everyone she loved—family members and friends? Would she ever see them again? She loved her friends and missed them terribly. She knew it was easier to do really scary and unpleasant things when your friends were around.

Her senses were more alert than ever. This was not like the rock climbing she'd done while attached to a harness. At the rock-climbing facility she'd visited with her brother, whenever someone had to let go while climbing, one of the trainers let the person down gently using the safety ropes. And she had never been good at rock climbing! She'd never reached the top, and she always ended up being rescued by the trainers after failing at each try. *Why am I thinking about this now? Do I want to fall?*

Rena inhaled a deep breath to calm her nerves. She pulled herself to another big ledge. She had to do this. She had to take the risk. She had to do this all on her own. If her mother could see her, she would be proud. At least that's what Rena thought. She pressed herself against the wall and moved carefully, inch by inch, stepping onto each new foothold as it came into view. She prayed that she would reach the top. She couldn't wait around for a rescue. *Sometimes a girl just has to rescue herself.*

Rena suddenly heard loud footsteps. They became louder as they got closer. Rena didn't know what was going on, but she knew she couldn't hide now. Where could she hide? How could she hide? She was clinging to a rock a few hundred feet up from the ground. She hoped she would blend in with the rock. She would be very still and hope that whoever was out there wouldn't notice her.

Rena pressed herself against the rock and tried her best not to stand out. Thoughts suddenly flashed in her head, and she thought about what was below her. What if there was a demon in this cave? What if he saw her? What would happen to her then? Panic overtook her, and she found herself looking down. She froze in fear. How on earth had she ever climbed up so far? *Get ahold of yourself! It doesn't matter how far it is! You'd just better not fall!* She took a few deep breaths. That helped calm her nerves. All she had to do was stay quiet.

With each passing moment, the footsteps became louder. They sounded like a drum. Then, all at once, the footsteps stopped. Whatever it was must be standing right under her; she could sense it. Her fears wouldn't leave her alone; they kept pinching at her skin and flying all around her like annoying little mosquitoes. No one ever likes those little creatures.

She wanted to look down. What was she thinking, looking down now? She knew it was a dumb idea, but she wanted to know what was below her. The small amount of light that shone through the ceiling should be enough for her to see properly. She moved her head and looked down. It was human. A human wearing furs. Could it be a caveman? Maybe she was in the time period when cavemen existed. She saw him sniffing the air. What was he doing?

Then, he suddenly looked up. Rena almost screamed when she saw him look her way. Instead, she pressed against the rock harder, which caused a small rock to fall to the ground. It hit the rock floor, and when it did, it sounded like a gunshot as it echoed throughout the whole cave.

"I know you're up there!" The man's voice echoed through the whole cave. "I know you're up there because I can smell your scent." *Smell my scent?*

Rena thought. *Then he can't be human. How can a human have such a good sense of smell? Then he must be a demon, but he looks so much like a human.*

"Come down from there!" he commanded.

"No!" she yelled back, trying to sound as if she wasn't scared.

"Get down here, or I'll come up and get you!"

"How? By the time you get up here, I'll already be to the top."

"Not if I do this!" He moved like a flash of lightening. He jumped on one ledge and then onto another with great speed. Rena thought, *How is this possible? This isn't humanly possible! Is he even human? If he isn't, then what is he?* Before she even had enough time to think about her situation, he was already on the same ledge she was on. Rena panicked. She let go and slowly started to fall. She screamed as she reached her hands out as if she was hoping that someone would take hold of them. *Is this how it's going to end?* She thought. *Is this how I will spend my last minutes on earth? I don't want to die!* "Someone please come," she whispered as she closed her eyes. "Someone please save me!"

Someone grabbed her hand and pulled her. Rena opened her eyes and saw the stranger pulling her back onto a lower ledge. She noticed that she had fallen a few feet down. Rena looked at the guy and felt grateful he was there; in fact, never had she felt so grateful toward someone. "I finally got you, you troublesome girl," he said.

Rena held on to him tightly because she was afraid that she might fall again. "Thank you," she said. What he did next brought tears to her eyes. He held onto her so tightly she winced. Then, all at once, he started jumping down from one ledge to another. Rena was too afraid to look down. She hid her face in the guy's fur jacket and did not look up until they stopped. When they were at the bottom, he brought Rena up to her feet. "Now," he said, "let's get to the point. Who are you, and how did you get inside this cave?"

She felt a little dizzy and found it difficult to stand up straight. Her feet and arms hurt more than ever now.

"Answer me!"

"I don't know! I don't know how I got here." Her mind was too fuzzy; she couldn't even think straight. "I was in the water … and then I ended up here." She looked up at the ceiling at the light. "I think through there," she said pointing.

He looked up and then understood. He smiled. "So you stumbled into this cave by mistake. Is that what you want to say?" Rena nodded. "Well, I'm sorry to tell you, girl, but this is a secret place, and I can't have you telling anyone about it."

"Huh? I won't tell anyone about it. I said I got here by accident. Why would I need to tell anyone about this place?"

"But how can I be sure I can trust you? You might be one of my enemies."

"What would I gain out of telling anyone about this place? It has nothing to do with me, and I came here for another reason."

"And what would that be?"

"I'm afraid I can't tell you."

"Why can't you tell me?"

Why doesn't he understand? she thought. *If I don't want to tell him, then he should leave the subject. Does he ever give up?* "Will you stop already? Why can't you understand that I don't want to tell you?"

He came close to her and gave her a serious look. "Look, girl, right now you're my prisoner, so you have to tell me anything I want to know. Got it?"

Rena looked into his eyes but did not say anything. He wasn't going to get anything out of her. Then, as if she had just noticed something about him she hadn't noticed before, she said,

"You're a hanta!" How on earth did she know something like this? How could she tell?

"Glad you noticed, little girl," he said with a smirk.

"How is it possible that you live in an underwater cave?" Rena found herself asking.

"I've been raised by wolves my whole life. It doesn't matter where I live as long we can survive. We are protected from our enemies."

"Cowards!" She found herself shouting. She felt angry about what he had said. Was this her or Sara? "Hantas are hunters," she said. "They are born free, born to hunt and kill their enemies, not hide away in caves! If you want to hunt you need to be hunted."

"You talk too much!" His face darkened, and she felt something dark and cold about him. *Why is she doing this?* He thought. *As I told her, she is my prisoner! She should keep her mouth shut if she wants to escape out of this cave alive.* Then he started to tell his story, which Rena found interesting. "I am the last of my kind," he said. "I live with wolves. You said I need to protect my family. I'm not going to let my family suffer because of my stupid mistakes." His tone changed; it grew colder. Rena felt cold, dark energy coming from him as he got close. She didn't feel anything. Her headache finally got to her, and she fell, hitting the cold stone floor.

***

How could I lose her? Thought Zidika. *How could something like this happen?* He wanted to protect her, to help her, be there for her. Now he was no longer that knight in shining armor, no longer the hero. How could he be a hero if he couldn't even protect a single girl? How could she depend on him to rescue her if he couldn't even look after her?

He swam into the water to where he had last seen her, but nothing was there. Nothing mattered to him except finding Rena. Where was she? "Rena, where are you!" he yelled as he searched. His thoughts were concentrated only on her. In his mind, he saw her scared and asking for help.

Zidika was so angry with himself that he could barely hold it back. It was going to lash out any minute if he didn't find some way to control it. His blood was boiling, his eyes changing. He tried to hold back as much as he could. He didn't want his anger to take control. Even the amulet couldn't help at this point. His insides were crushing him as he assumed the worst. *She's dead.*

No, she's not. She's not dead!

This girl was strong. He knew that. But sometimes she looked so weak and helpless. After all, she was the one who had come to him for help. He should never have said yes. He should have said no. Stupid girl! What a joke. She had trusted him. Why?

She made him feel happy. He had fun with her. All these emotions flowed all at once inside him. He wanted to push her away, yet at the same time pull her closer. He prayed that she was all right and safe. He prayed that he would be able to get to her in time before anything bad happened. No matter what, he would save her. He would get to her, and they would make it out of whatever place she was in.

He had to focus. He had to look harder. Why did it bother him so much that she was gone? They had been traveling together for only a short time. Soon she would leave. He promised himself that he would protect her till then. Why had he become so attached to her? After Sara went away, he swore that he would never let a girl get close to him. Maybe it was because Sara was inside of her. No, that wasn't it. He had wanted her way before he knew about that.

"You will find the thing you are looking for." Those had been her last words. His heart had shattered when she disappeared. She was important to him. Actually, Rena was more than important. He trusted her, even though she hadn't told him the whole truth. Trust was important in a relationship. "I'll find you, Rena. I'll find you!" he shouted.

CHAPTER 11

Kari Kaia

. . . .

It was cold in the cell, really cold. Rena lay down, closing her eyes for a bit, until her pain caused her to sit up. She remained silent. Motionless. She didn't care about anything—not even where she was. She had lost hope. She sat in her cell pathetically, but she didn't dare cry. She didn't want to show the slightest fear—or any emotion. She had no energy left. She only sat there and waited till her time came. She didn't care about anything anymore. She went into silent mode as she entered her own world again where only she existed, where she floated on air and didn't care about the rest of the world, where she became her silent reflection. Until a voice brought her back.

"Why are you being like this?" Sara asked in a worried tone. "You were finally coming out of your shell, and now after everything that happened, at a time like this, you go back in. Rena, remember what you can do. Remember what you came here for. You're a strong girl, and you can't lose hope this easily."

Sara's voice made Rena feel better; it reminded her of her responsibility. "You're right." Rena spoke happily. "I did all this work, and I'm not going to lose now. I have a few tricks up my sleeve and, as well, I have a power of my own." She stood up and walked to the bars of the cell. Rena stretched both hands forward and took hold of the bars. Suddenly they turned into solid ice. "Don't mess with me!" Rena yelled as she lifted up her foot kicked the bars. They shattered into tiny pieces.

Once out, Rena hurried to find a way to escape that place. Climbing again was definitely not an option. It was too dark to see anything, yet Rena used one of her five senses to find a way out. Until she heard a voice. It sounded like a girl, and she was softly weeping. The sound seemed to be coming from one of the other cells, and so Rena followed the sounds. When she came to the girl's cell, Rena took hold of the bars and turned them into ice. She blew her icy breath to help the metal crack and shatter into many pieces.

The girl stopped weeping. "Who is it? Who's here?" she said in a scared and lonely voice.

"Do not be afraid," Rena said walking in. "I'm not going to hurt you." For some reason Rena could now see a little better, as if she had night vision. She saw the girl in the far corner of the cell. Her dress was torn into rags and her hair was tied back into a messy bun. Her bangs covered her eyes. "Why did you come here?" asked the girl.

Rena walked up to the girl and knelt down in front of her. The girl turned away as Rena tried to see her clearly. "Let me see you," she said gently.

"As I asked before, why have you come here?"

"Isn't it obvious? I have come to save you."

But the girl did not look happy; instead she looked even more bitter. "Why?" she said in an icy could voice. "Don't you know who I am? You should be afraid of me."

"And why would I be afraid of you?"

But then the girl's voice only sounded more bitter. "I'm a demon! A worthless human who has been cursed with powers I do not understand."

Rena only smiled because she understood now why this girl was so bitter toward her.

When the girl saw Rena smiling, her face grew colder and her eyes looked ice cold. "Why would you come to save me? Why are you smiling as if it's something to be proud of? I'm an outcast. Even people in my own village didn't want me. How can you know anything about it?"

Her words were a lie. Rena tried to look into her eyes to see the true emotions that she was hiding, because words may lie but eyes can't. "I never said I did." The girl looked at Rena in anger. "But the reason I'm smiling is that I know where you're coming from." The girl looked a Rena in surprise, but she did not show any signs of happiness. "It's nothing to be ashamed of. Instead you should be proud that you possess this kind of a gift."

"A gift?"

"Yes! You're not the only person who has this kind of power. Many women like you possess strange powers that they are afraid of and don't know what to do with. Because they think of the power as a threat, they run away from it. But that is not the case. The truth is, you can be using this power to help yourself, to protect you and the people you love. You can use your power to save your village whenever a demon may attack. You live in an era in which lots of demons prey on humans. Am I right?" The girl nodded, amazed at Rena's speech. "You can use your power to protect your village, you see? It is not something you should be afraid of." Rena smiled a bright smile and held out a hand. "Come with me." The girl grabbed her hand, and as she stood up, she pushed her hair out of her eyes. Her eyes shone with happiness, as if hope had been brought back to her. "You can also tell the same to other people who think their power is a curse."

The girl smiled at Rena. She loosened her bun, and her brown hair fell over her shoulders. "Yes, you have given me hope again, and so I shall do the same for others."

"Let's go," Rena said taking her hand.

"Be careful! There is a hunter here with a pack of wolves. They can hear and sense anything."

"Yeah, I already met that jerk," Rena said angrily as she remembered her own experience.

They tried to sneak out of the cave quietly without being seen or heard. But it was all in vain. When they heard howling, they soon realized they that they were surrounded by wolves. A lit torch appeared in front of them, and the hunter stood there pointing an arrow at them. Rena stood in front of the girl. Now that she could see his face a little better, she was surprised at what he looked like. He wasn't at all what she had expected him to be. She expected a man in his thirties with a beard, but he looked closer to eighteen. His face could be described as handsome. He had dark-brown eyes and really dark hair. His skin was pale, but he seemed to have a little tan. Everything about him screamed "bad boy."

Rena held her breath. She didn't want to show any signs of fear. She remained motionless. "Nice power you have," he told them. "But it won't get you out of here." Then he noticed the girl with Rena and was amazed that she had been able to escape as well since she was the one who had asked to be locked up and maybe even killed.

"Thanks, but I'll take my chances," Rena said as she and the girl backed away, their backs facing each other. Rena whispered, "Okay, girl, use your powers and take the wolves. I'll deal with the hunter."

The girl nodded. "Good thinking," said the girl. "Try to distract him so he won't be able to help the wolves. I'll burn them to a crisp."

Rena's eyes widened as she remembered the hunter saying that they were his only family, and the only reason they hid out here in this underwater cave was to protect the last remaining of his kind. "No! Don't do that. Just knock them out. That should give us plenty of time to escape." The girl nodded once more.

"Okay, now!" Rena shouted. She ran forward toward the hunter. Pulling out her sword, Rena struck out at him, but she missed her mark. He used his arm to block the blow, and soon took hold of the sword and threw it away from them where it soon disappeared.

The girl's hands flared up. She lunged fire balls at the wolves, and they backed away a few feet. Then she ran toward Rena, her feet emitting fire with every step.

Rena, on the other hand, was not in such a good position. She tried to hit the hunter again, but he ducked. He tried to hit her, and she ducked. But he grabbed her hand. "Let me go!" Rena yelled. She was angry. She didn't want him to see her as the helpless little girl he thought she was. She was going to prove him wrong. "Let go!" she kicked him in the knee. He backed away, still holding her. The anger was boiling within her. She couldn't handle this. Maybe she had been wrong. Maybe she needed Zidika after all. Maybe she could not do this on her own.

All of a sudden, Rena's hands seemed to be lit on fire. She screamed, but then she realized that it wasn't burning her. It was on her side. She watched as the girl fought. For someone who was afraid of her own power was really good at this. Rena raised hands and started shooting fire at him. All of a sudden, she couldn't control her power. It was too strong for her. Soon the place tuned into a fire pit. Fire engulfed everything. Bits of Rena's hair turned red, and steam was actually coming out of her ears. Rena opened her mouth to speak, but all that came out were puffs of smoke. *What is going on?* Rena thought as she was shooting fire out of her hands, and everything in sight was bathed in fire. She couldn't control it. The fire was like an unwilling beast that didn't want to be tamed. She couldn't stop it.

All the wolves scattered like ants. The girl stopped and looked at Rena, amazed that Rena had so much power. The hunter was nowhere to be seen. "You're a kari kaia as well," said the girl. "That is awfully strange because it's not known for a human to possess two of the powers. You're a fire bender," the girl said.

"It would be nice if you could help me here and not tell me stories," Rena said, trying not to choke from the smoke invading her lungs.

The girl used her hands to cover her mouth. "Fire is a really difficult element to control. If you don't use it right, it will destroy you and everything it sees. But if you learn how to use it and communicate with it, it can be the most beautiful thing you've ever seen."

"Tell me how to stop it!"

"You must learn how to communicate with it. Learn the proper way to use it. You must listen to it."

"And how am I supposed to do that?"

"Close your eyes and concentrate on the power." It was Sara speaking. Rena did as she was told. "Good. Free your mind from everything. Just relax. Don't worry about this right now. Just relax. Don't think about anything. Concentrate and relax. Don't be afraid. Fire is an element that can destroy and can hurt people. But without fire we wouldn't be able to survive. Fire is both destructive *and* beautiful." Rena listened to Sara and let her voice guide her. She was starting to understand what Sara was saying. Her words calmed her down like a soothing waterfall. She no longer felt the burning sensation in her lungs. She didn't feel as if her ears were burning off. As she kept her eyes closed, she saw beautiful lights. She opened her eyes and saw the flames in green, blue, and yellow. Lights were twirling alongside the flames. It was truly fascinating. She stared at it as if she had been waiting her whole life for this. But still there was one problem remaining. The fire hadn't died out. The smoke was spreading everywhere, and soon it would take its toll on both Rena and the girl unless she did something, and quickly.

Rena put her hands together and tried to imagine a waterfall. She thought about the calming waters bathing her, relaxing her, freeing her mind, and letting her concentrate. Suddenly, water started leaking from the cracks in the cave, and within seconds she and the girl were completely surrounded by water, as if they were out in the ocean. Rena opened her eyes and struggled to swim up, but then she realized she didn't need to because somehow she could breathe underwater. She looked over to the girl to see if she was all right and saw that she was okay. Rena felt relieved and happy. Now she had to figure out a way to get out of this mess.

The hunter was gone, and so were the wolves. This was their perfect opportunity to escape. Rena forced her hands apart, and soon the water vanished. Both the girl and Rena fell to the ground, breathing heavily. "It's amazing," the girl managed to say. "You possess all three powers—ice, water, and fire. It is so amazing. Who are you?"

"Yes, Rena." It was Sara again. "It is very unusual for a woman to possess all three powers ... unless you are—"

Just then Sara broke all connection with Rena. Rena no longer heard her. The hunter returned with something in his hands—an orb. Bluish color circled around it like water—a storm twirling until it reached its limit. He held it in front of her. Rena froze. Her eyes went blank. The orb was sending images right to her head. It was showing her a story, telling her the past.

"What did you do?" the girl shouted. Rena heard voices in the background, but it all sounded blurry, fuzzy. The girl walked up to Rena and grabbed her arm. Rena did not respond. The girl looked at the hunter, furious. "Tell me! What did you do to her?" she said her hands flaring up.

In a few minutes, Rena saw the whole history of the wolf demon's tribe. She saw how they had survived and how they had managed to keep people from finding them, because they were considered evil. Why was he showing her this? What was the point of all of this?

The orb soon released its grip on Rena. The vivid color returned back to her eyes, and she could move. The bits of red that colored her hair still remained, but were reduced to a fraction of the color. The girl was about to run forward at the hunter when Rena stopped her. Rena fell to her knees. The stranger went up to her. "What does this mean?" Rena asked. The girl helped Rena get up. Rena looked up at him. He no longer looked as if he wanted to hurt her.

"This orb holds our tribe's history. It is the only thing that keeps us connected with Hina, goddess of the moon."

"I see what you mean," said Rena. "But what does this have to do with me?"

"Because I was born among the wolves, I was able to learn their language and I am able to communicate with them. I can speak to them, and they can speak to me. Our tribe leader told us about a girl who would save our tribe, a girl who's very powerful, a girl who has the will to fight. She has a fighting power within her. And when your fire power came, I knew you were the one. It is strange. Earlier I had a feeling that you might be the one he was talking about. He said that, if anyone like that came, I must take her as my wife."

"Wife! Who on earth do you think I am? I am not your Hina! I'm not a goddess of the moon! No! I'm not the girl you're looking for. There are lots of girls out there who are braver then I am. Even if I was the exact person your tribe leader said I am, I wouldn't be able to stay. The reason I came here was to find someone." She gasped. She finally had told him her purpose. She hadn't been planning to, but he had made her so mad that, for one second, she'd wanted to burn him to a crisp. This had been her secret. How dare he force her to tell him!

"You don't get it!" he responded. "You're the only one who can save us."

"What does it have to do with me?"

"You see, you're the onile."

"Onile? But doesn't that mean earth sprit?"

"Yes, but it also has a different meaning. It means chosen."

Rena's eyes flared up. He was making her angry. "What on earth are you talking about? Chosen? You must have me confused with someone else. I am not that girl. I came here only to get someone. I have seen this situation in many movies. People always tell others that they are the chosen ones, that they must save the world. Well, I'm not that person. Why is this happening to me? I didn't ask for this. Don't confuse me with someone else!" She started panicking and yelling until the girl's arm on her shoulder brought her back.

"Calm down," the girl said. "When he said the chosen one, he didn't actually mean some kind of savor destined to save our world. What he truly meant is that you're a very special girl, that you have been brought here for a specific reason, and that you must fulfill that reason—whatever it is."

"My reason?" Rena asked. The girl nodded. "What is my reason for being here?"

"Sorry if I might have upset you," the hunter said. "But would you mind telling me, who is this person you speak of?"

"My brother, Joey, was possessed by a centipede that kidnapped him and brought here. I'm here to find him and bring him back home."

"Why do you have to go home? Just stay here."

Rena gave him a dangerous look. How dare he even mention something like that? Was this guy trying to pick a fight with her? "How could you say that? If your tribe leader or anyone in your tribe got hurt, or someone was going to take a tribe member's life, wouldn't you do anything to try to help? That's how much he means to me. It's not as if he got into a car accident and he died and I'll never get to see him again. I have a chance to turn things around, to make things right. I have a chance to save him, and I will do anything in my power to do that." She started tearing up.

The hunter stared at her. The girl tried to calm Rena down. Then the hunter came up to her and took hold of her hands. "Your hands are so warm. Don't ever lose this warm feeling, no matter what you're going through." Rena pulled her hands free and then hugged him. "I know how you feel," continued the hunter. My brother and sisters were taken away by demons or humans. It was hard dealing with it." Rena looked up at him. "But I won't give up on you. I don't care if there are a million other girls who are braver and smarter. I will still make you mine one day."

"Oh, thanks. Is that supposed to make me feel better?" she said sarcastically. Then something got though her head. Why did you treat me like a prisoner, and now you want me to be your wife?"

"Well, I didn't know if I could trust you."

"Now you do?"

"Yeah."

She nudged him playfully on the shoulder. "Anyway, thanks."

"For what?"

"For not locking me up in a cage again." She gave him a bright and heartwarming smile. He found himself staring. "But there is something I want to know. Why did you lock her up?" She pointed at the girl.

The hunter looked at her, not surprised. "She was the one who came to me. She asked me to lock her up in a cell because she was afraid and didn't want to hurt anyone. So I did as she asked. Still, I was confused by her reasons because she never really explained. I was about to refuse, but—" He stopped and didn't finish his sentence. Then he grabbed Rena's hand. "Come on. I'll show you a way out." Rena smiled but pulled her hand back. She looked at the girl. She held her hand out to the girl. "Let's go." The girl looked as if she was a bit scared to grab her hand, but then she stepped out of the darkness smiling. She grabbed Rena's hand, and they both followed the hunter out.

He led them to the bottom of a cliff. They stopped. The hunter stood between them and grabbed both of their hands. They were both surprised when they all suddenly went speeding up the cliff. When they reached the top, Rena tried to calm her spinning head. The girl came up to Rena. She smiled in a way Rena hadn't seen before. Then they both turned to the hunter. "Thank you," said Rena. "Without your help, we may have never gotten out." They both smiled at him sweetly.

The girl turned to Rena. "I've got to tell you something," she said. "What I said about my village kicking me out isn't true. The truth is that I ran away. My sister must be angry because she was the only person I told about my power, and she told me not to be afraid, that everything would be all right. I'm sorry I lied to you."

"I'm not angry. At least you told me the truth now."

The girl smiled more brightly. "Well, I've got to go now," said the girl. "I have to return to my village. If there is any way I can help you, please let me know."

Rena walked up to her and put on hand on her shoulder. Her skin was so warm in the sun. "Promise me that you will try to help many girls who also have these powers and are afraid of them. Tell them that they do not have to be afraid."

The girl smiled back at Rena. "Of course." Then she paused. She gave Rena a bit of a worried look as if she was afraid to ask her something. "Hey, Rena, will you please help me with something?"

"What is it?"

"It's about a friend. She was taken away by some strangers who came to our village. Please, if you can, would you save her?"

Rena knew that she had to search for her brother, but inside she just couldn't refuse. "Yes, but I can't make any promises that I will bring her back safely."

"At least I will know that you will try to save her."

Rena smiled sweetly at the girl and then she looked out into the open sea, her imagination lost in the waters that were crashing against the rocks.

"Their village is over there at the west side of Nippon." The hunter looked at her. "If you're looking for a centipede, you'd better go to the west side of Nippon. There you might be able to find what you're looking for."

Rena smiled brightly at him. "Thanks. I hope we will meet again someday."

"Don't worry. We will."

"What do you mean?"

"As you said before, I live to hunt and kill, so I'm going out to do just that. We might meet again some time later."

"Yes, I think we will. Thanks a lot." She turned back to the girl. "Well, I guess this is where we say goodbye." She wanted to shake hands with her, but instead she hugged her.

"Thank you so much," the girl said, and it almost sounded as if she was crying.

"Oh, I never got your name."

"It's Rin. Oh, and thank you so much. You don't know how much it means."

They both waved goodbye and left in opposite directions. As Rena drew her attention back to the ocean, wind twirled around her and prickled her skin. Then, off to the right, she saw Zidika. He seemed to be out of breath.

CHAPTER 12

Those Eyes

• • • • • • • • • • •

Zidika's blood turned cold. He was angry. Angry to the point that he could no longer contain himself. "Rena!"

Zidika's voice had lost all its warmth, and Rena was starting to get a bit worried. His eyes danced in a dangerous anger. Rena had never seen him like this, and she became more worried as the silence grew.

"Here I am worrying about you," he said, "and you were up here enjoying yourself!"

For some odd reason, his words stung her, but she didn't show it. "Zidika, you don't know what I've been through just now, so don't you even dare accuse me of something, because I didn't do anything wrong." She spoke in a high-pitched voice. But her words just made him angrier. Rena swore she saw his eyes turn red—from a hazel green to a bright red, the same color her brother's eyes had been when he was possessed.

A hurricane of flashbacks erupted in her head. Her eyes widened. She felt her insides tear up at what she suddenly realized at that moment. She stood frozen. No, she couldn't let it happen, not again. She couldn't let someone she cared about be taken away by those big blood eyes.

"Are you listening to me?" Zidika spoke in a harsh tone.

Rena tore herself away from life and fell to her knees, her arms hugging herself. "No, no no …" she repeated again and again. "I'm not going to let this happen again. I couldn't stop it when it did happen, but I can do something about it now." She spoke in a scared voice, as if she seen a ghost. Her eyes showed fear, and she was trembling.

Zidika's red eyes faded, and he looked at the girl in front of him. All his bad feeling evaporated as he saw her on her knees before him. What was he doing? Why had he let himself get so angry? It was her life. She could do whatever she wanted. What did it matter to him? Yet, was it wrong to worry about her? But as he looked at Rena, his heart broke with everything that had happened. He wanted to be by her side. Taking in a deep breath he walked toward her.

"I couldn't stop him," she said, looking up at him. Soon she broke into tears.

Zidika saw the sadness and loneliness in her eyes. "Rena, I'm—"

"Zidika, don't leave me!" She sobbed loudly as she clung onto Zidika as if her life depended on him. "I couldn't stop him from leaving! I couldn't do anything!" Her grasp on his arm tightened. "I tried, but in the end, he still left." Now she wasn't talking only about Joey. She tore herself away from him. "So, promise you won't leave me. Promise you'll stay with me till the end. Till I at least find my brother." She continued to sob.

"Rena," he said, pulling her back to him. Rena nested her head in his chest. "Remember what I said. I'll never leave you. I'll stay by your side."

"Really?" she mumbled, looking up at him. Her eyes and nose were running, her checks were rosy, and her eyes were puffy.

He pulled her back into his chest, stroking her hair gently. "Rena, I promise that, till we find your brother, you can count on me to be there for you." Rena felt calm as her tears stopped.

CHAPTER 13

Brother

· · · · · · · ·

"We have to travel to the west side of Nippon. I was told that I may be able to get some information there."

"You do realize that we will have to travel a long distance from here to there."

"Yes, it would be easier if we could get some horses to ride."

"Why horses when we can ride a dragon?"

"A dragon …?" Her voice trailed off, and she found herself amazed at what he had said.

"I would prefer a dragon, wouldn't you? It will be much quicker."

"A dragon," she said nervously. "I've always heard myths about dragons. I've heard that they are very dangerous creatures."

"Oh, no. Then you must have heard it wrong. They can be the most gentle and loyal animal species in the world. But there is one thing that you need to know about them before going to search for one."

"What?"

"A dragon has to recognize you as its owner before you can ride it. Otherwise, it will burn you to a crisp."

"Well, thanks for telling me that, Captain Obvious." She sneered in a playful way, turning away and heading back to their campsite.

Before the day ended, Rena remembered the promise she had made to Rin. She thought that maybe Zidika didn't need to know, but he had been so kind by agreeing to help her, he at least deserved to know what she was planning to do next.

The next day, they headed out to another village to get horses and information about dragons. They had forgotten about the island of demons, since it was obviously the wrong place to look. They walked into a rich village. It was market day, and tables were set out laden with goods for sale—jewelry, perfume, dresses, food, and other things that people might find useful. People walked among the tables looking at the merchandise. They stared at Rena, and Rena gave them a look before turning her attention back to the tables. Something caught Rena's eye, and she walked over to a table and looked at the red globe on display. Picking it up, Rena felt a spark of electricity jolt into her. She almost dropped the ball when it shocked her for an instant. The ball was filled with some unusual shades, most of them red. She saw orange, dark red, bright red, yellow, and other colors that couldn't be described. All these colors were mixed together in that orb. It caught her attention, and it seemed as if it wouldn't let her go. She stared at it with great interest until the vendor broke that hold. "Miss, would you like to buy this?" Rena missed what the guy had said and focused her attention on the orb. It seemed it didn't want to let her go. It was taking her over just as that blue orb in the cave had done.

Zidika had finished asking for horses and saw Rena staring blankly at the sphere. He knew something must be wrong. He walked over to her, breaking her concentration. "Rena, what is that?" he asked.

Rena turned away from the orb and looked at Zidika. He noticed that something was wrong. He looked into her eyes and saw that they had turned a little red. Rena stared blankly at him.

"Miss, would you like to buy this?" the vendor asked again. Rena turned back to him and gave him a bitter smile. He didn't seem to notice it. He didn't see anything wrong with her. Was Zidika the only one who could tell that something was wrong?

"Yes," she finally answered. "How much will it be?"

"Rena, we've already spend a lot on the horses," Zidika warned. "We can't spend more on useless stuff."

Rena turned around, anger in her eyes. "Who says this is useless?" she yelled. "This may not be important to you, but for me it damn sure is!" The village people who had been looking around the place stopped and stared at the two people who were making a scene.

"Okay," Zidika said. "Maybe it's not so useless, but I'm not sure we have enough money to buy something like that. I've already bought two horses and a map. I don't think I will have enough."

But the vendor interrupted them. "If you want it, I can give it to you for cheap."

Rena turned to face him. "How much do you want?" she asked again.

"Two gold pieces."

Zidika reached into his pocket and pulled out two gold coins. He handed them to Rena. She took them without hesitation and handed them to the vendor. She took the orb in her hands, looking at it intensely. The vendor tried to get Rena's attention, but she ignored him. Zidika approached the vendor and took the bag that came with the orb. Zidika told Rena to put the orb in the bag, but she refused. She didn't want to let it out of her sight. People kept staring at them as they passed. What was so interesting about them? Why did they have to stare? Didn't they realize it was rude?

As Rena and Zidika walked to the stable to pick out their horses, they passed three young women who appeared to be about sixteen years old. They wore brightly colored dresses. One of them wore a light-green dress with a dark belt tied around her waist. One was dressed in pink while the other wore a white dress. They looked at Rena's clothes and laughed. "What is this? A freak show?" one of them said as she laughed with the other two.

Rena finally tore her gaze from the orb. She gave it to Zidika and looked at the girls with flaring eyes. The red color started invading her hair, turning bits of it dark red. Her eyes seemed to burn with fire in them. "Who you calling a freak show?" she said, about to explode.

The girls looked at her, shocked by her sudden change, but then the shock expired, and they started laughing at her again. "You, of course," said the girl in the pink dress. "Who else do you see here wearing such strange clothes? I would be embarrassed to be seen anywhere with you." Then they spotted Zidika.

The girl in the flirty green dress, who seemed to be the leader, went up to him and started talking to him. "Hey, what are you doing hanging out with her? Drop her and come hang out with us," she said, taking his hand.

Zidika removed her hand and stepped back. "I'm sorry, girls, but I'm already taken." The girl looked at him in amazement as she turned to Rena. "You mean you're with her? This freak show?" she screamed her eyes flaring with anger. Then she smiled a bit before she tore her gaze away from Rena. "Oh, I don't see what could be wrong if you hung out with us." She tried to plant a kiss on his cheek, but he moved out of the way, and she almost fell to the ground. The other two girls snickered.

"Sorry," Zidika said in a not-so-apologetic tone.

The girl got up and giggled rather stupidly. "Come on! You don't have to play hard to get." She leaned in and placed a quick kiss on his check. Zidika didn't even try to stop her. The other two girls, upon seeing this, quickly turned to look at Rena to see how she would react.

Zidika's action had hurt her in more ways than one. She couldn't control her anger. "That's it!" she yelled. Her eyes were literally on fire, and her hair had turned dark red—it was the color of blood! She began to dance rhythmically. Feeling her anger coming to a boil, she held out her hands out. A lightning bolt combined with fire shot from her fingers and headed straight for the girl. The girl didn't move. She was too frightened, too shocked, too amazed that Rena was able to do that. This time she really had messed with the wrong girl, and she was going to pay for that painfully.

Zidika pushed the girl out of the way just before the lightning bolt hit her. Instead, it hit the side of the wooden stable, but the fire didn't burn out. The blue and red color remained. It turned black soon, but still didn't die out. It devoured half of the wall before Rena combined both of her powers and finally caused the fire to die out.

Rena still looked at the girls in anger. Zidika and the girl stood up. "I suggest you leave," said Rena. "I never want to see your faces again. If I do, it will be too soon." The girl backed away from Zidika, and the other two ran up to her. The three of them quickly hurried away. Rena turned to Zidika, her eyes still on fire. "Why did you stop her?" she shouted.

Zidika didn't say a word. "Let's go get our horses," he said as he turned and walked to the shed.

After a while, Rena calmed herself down. She felt like a totally different person when she was holding the orb. She hated the anger. She walked into the shed, and her eyes settled on the most beautiful creatures she had ever seen. "These are our horses?" Rena looked at all the beautiful animals.

"Do you want ordinary horses or unicorns?" asked Zidika. "You can pick any animal here that you want."

"Thank you, Zidika," said Rena, and she ran off to look at the other horses and unicorns.

CHAPTER 14

The Crying Unicorn

· ·

Rena walked around in the shed for at least an hour. There were just so many horses and unicorns to choose from. They all looked so beautiful and gentle. They were magnificent. They all wore necklaces of flowers around their necks. All the flowers were different colors and smelled amazing.

One unicorn wore flowers of different colors. This was the unicorn that caught Rena's eye. She was more beautiful than all the others, and Rena would have picked her right away except that she had been put in the back of the stable where no one could see her. Rena wondered why such a beautiful animal had been put in such a dark and lonely place. She should have been with the others, where everybody could see her and be impressed with her beauty.

Rena walked over to the white unicorn with pink hooves and flowing blond mane and tail. The flowers around her neck were white roses, and the smell delighted Rena. As Rena walked up to the creature that was the fairest of them all, the stunning creature backed away from her. Rena didn't understand, and she moved even closer. The unicorn stomped and backed up again, but Rena remained on her spot. She knew what was going on, and she wanted to get closer to the unicorn. The unicorn jumped and kicked and backed away, warning her to stay away. But Rena continued to move forward. The unicorn whinnied and kicked forward, just missing Rena. Rena backed away a little, but then she saw something. There were tears in the unicorn's eyes. Rena wondered why a gorgeous creature such as this animal would be crying. "Why are you crying?" Rena asked, reaching her hand out to touch the unicorn's muzzle.

The unicorn stopped jumping and looked at Rena. "You can see my tears?" The unicorn spoke in such a beautiful voice. It sounded almost as if she was singing in an angel's voice.

Rena had not expected an answer because she didn't think that animals talked, but apparently it was just the natural thing to do. "Yes, I could. Now tell me why such a stunning creature like you would be crying."

"It is said that humans cannot see a unicorn's tears. Why is it that you can?"

Rena smiled sweetly at the creature. "I just can."

"I'm Celesta. I'm crying because I don't belong. I'm not free. I was taken from my home and put into this place, and I must remain here until someone comes to get me. I try to scare anyone who tries to get near me. You're a brave girl. The humans do not know I can speak." Celesta smiled and let Rena pet her. "I do not belong here, and neither do these other unicorns, but they do not mind staying here. They are happy, and I can respect that. It's just that I don't want to be bought. I want to be free and roam the fields like I was meant to."

Rena knew that she had to do something to help this beautiful creature. "You're such a beautiful unicorn. Tears aren't meant for you. I'll grant you your wish."

"You will? Thank you." Joy sprang into her voice.

"Just don't say anything until we are far from the village." Rena didn't want anyone to notice and then try to take the unicorn away from her. Rena smiled brightly. She put a halter on the unicorn and led her out of the building, happy to own such an amazing animal. She walked up to Zidika smiling brightly as if her day couldn't get any better, as if she had forgotten about everything that had happened on that day. "I'm taking this one," she told him.

Zidika tuned around to look at the horse she had picked. He was stunned at how beautiful the animal was. "Wow! She's gorgeous!" The unicorn stood next to Rena. They made a great pair, as if Rena was destined to be her rider. This animal was all white with pink hooves.

The way Zidika was looking at her made Rena's insides turn warm. He had never looked at her like that before. So … what was it? It was as if he had feelings for her. It made her turn away in embarrassment. She frowned at her next thought. He would never have feelings for her because he had feelings for Sara. It had been written all over his face the last time he talked with Sara. How could he ever have feelings for her? Who was she to him? She was nothing to him, just a wandering girl who came out of the forest, a lost and scared girl who knew nothing at his way of living, someone who was a total stranger to him. He would always see her as just a friend—always a friend. It was now that she accepted that nothing more would never happen. They would always be friends. She needed to start looking at him as a friend and nothing more.

But it was hard holding secrets from her best friend. He was a friend she trusted so much more than anyone she had ever trusted before. Oh, how many times had she wanted to confess to him? How many times had she wanted to tell him about everything? She had daydreamed about this. He made her feel happy. Zidika filled a part of her heart she never knew existed. And this quickly, she had fallen for this guy. She had known him for only two weeks. But he had said and done so much for her. He had saved her several times. It was hard to not fall for a guy who had saved her life more than once. Being saved by a guy was way more romantic than receiving roses from him. Still, it had hurt to find out that the guy she loved was in love with someone else. That was horrible news. Rena had never wanted to get involved in this kind of mess; she never thought she would. But she couldn't stay away from him. She wanted to see him.

She tried to imagine her life without him. What would it be like after their mission was over? She wouldn't be able to handle it easily; her heart was hurting. How was she supposed to forget about him if she always kept thinking about him? Maybe it would be okay if they just remained only friends. That might be fine. Maybe she wasn't ready to become more than friends with Zidika. If she became too attached to Zidika, if they became more than friends, how would she handle it? Would she be able to handle it? She was only fourteen, but he was different from anyone she had ever met. If he ever asked her to stay, she might even stay. What was she thinking? How could she stay when she had to take her brother home? If only Zidika was from the future—from her world—things would be so much simpler.

She remembered how she felt when she first saw him and when they first talked. She remembered what she felt at the time. She didn't have these feelings she was feeling for him now. She wondered what he felt for her, what he thought about her, what he saw in her that he hadn't seen in any other girls. She knew that he thought of her differently. She saw that in his eyes. She knew that he saw her as different. She wished he thought of her a little more. When they first met, he had acted a bit rude. He might even have kicked her out the next day if she hadn't gone out of her way to help him. But then something about him changed overnight. He started to act much sweeter to her even way before he found out that Sara was with her. But maybe if he didn't know about Sara, maybe, just maybe, he might have fallen for her.

Rena's heart starting pounding against her chest in worry. This was going to be harder than she thought. She had to get away. If she didn't, she wouldn't be sure what she should do next. Would she be able to control her emotions?

She thought that, maybe, she would even choose to stay with Zidika and send Joey back home by himself. She shook the thought out of her head. How could she think of something so selfish? What would everyone think? What would they do without her? Mom would be heartbroken for losing someone she cared for. Her friends—she thought about them the most for some reason. They would change. She noticed that right away about them. They were different than she thought, and that's what made them so interesting. If she was gone, they would change so much. Everyone would change. She needed to stop thinking about this. She had a duty to fulfill, and she didn't need to fill her head with worry.

"I picked this one." Zidika pointed to a brown horse with black mane and tail. Zidika's choice finally got Rena out of her head and enabled her to concentrate on the present. She took a deep breath and looked at the horse he had pointed to. She was amazed at his choice. Out of all the unicorns he could have chosen, he had chosen a regular horse. "Really? You picked this one? From all the beautiful unicorns, you pick a normal-looking plain horse?"

"Unicorns are much faster," Celesta said. "Better if there is somewhere you have to be quickly."

Rena gave her a stare. "I told you not speak till we are out of the village." Celesta looked down as if she was ashamed. "Well," said Rena, "you heard her. Go pick out a unicorn. They are much faster." Rena spoke in a commanding voice.

Zidika stood there speechless. He had lived in this place for three years, and he didn't know that some of the animals could talk. Maybe he should try talking with the cats when he got back to his house.

Rena waited for him outside for ten minutes while the stable manager helped her saddle the unicorn. Zidika came out with a unicorn that didn't look much different from the horse he had picked before. It was black and had white dots on its butt and long, dark mane and tail. White flowers had been woven into his mane. Still, he looked beautiful.

Zidika helped Rena get onto her unicorn and then got onto his. Rena pulled of the flower necklace off the unicorn's neck and put it in her backpack along with the orb. "Why would you need those?" Celesta asked.

"I may want to decorate your mane later," she said, smiling.

Celeta smiled back. "I'd like that," she said, and she started to run.

Inside Rena's pack, the orb suddenly shone bright, turning the flowers into a bloody red color.

CHAPTER 15

In the Dragon's Cave

· · · · · · · · · · · · · · · ·

Rena had never ridden a horse before, except for one time when her class visited a stable on a school field trip. That time she had to ride with a teacher and not by herself. So now it was pretty hard for her to adjust and get used to the saddle and the unicorn running like the wind. On the other hand, the two unicorns loved this freedom. They loved racing against the wind, their manes flying in the air and the cold piercing their skin. "This is amazing," Celesta told Rena. "I feel free when I'm running with the wind. You don't know how long I have waited for this moment."

"I'm glad you're happy," Rena said petting the unicorn's neck. "You don't mind me sitting on your back?"

"Hey, as long as my owner allows me to feel as if I'm free, I'm happy, and I don't mind."

Rena looked at Zidika to see his reaction, but then she felt guilty for not telling him where they were going to go first. She still wondered. She wanted to ask. As much as it hurt her, she needed to ask him.

"Rena!" Zidika shouted. "We getting close to the dragon's cave." Celesta suddenly stopped. Zidika's unicorn stopped too. Rena almost flew out of the saddle. "What's this about a dragon's cave?" Celesta spoke almost in anger.

"Celesta, we are traveling to find a dragon. It is said that dragons are the fastest creatures and that they know a lot. Even through you are fast, we can't afford to waste a lot of time."

"You don't need me," said Celesta. "Why didn't you at least tell me where we were going? I could have at least warned you that we can't go."

"What do you mean, you can't go? Why?" Now she was angry, but she tried to keep it under control. She counted to ten, and her anger slowly evaporated.

"We are the enemies of dragons. Dragons hate us because we are the only creatures that can kill them. We have killed many of their kind." Now Rena's anger returned. Now that they were so close, they learned that their rides were the enemies of the dragons.

"If they see us," said Zidika's unicorn, "they won't hesitate to burn you to ashes."

"I'm sorry Rena," said Celesta. "We are the natural enemies of these dragons. I wish things could change between us, but they can't." Tears appeared in Celesta's eyes.

But Rena was no longer angry. Rena got out of her saddle and hugged Celesta her and petted her beautiful blond mane. Rena remembered her promise to the unicorn. "Celesta, I told you that I would set you free, and I will do that. If you do not want to come with me, you are free to go."

Celesta put her muzzle on Rena's shoulder. "Are you sure?" she said looking at Rena.

Rena touched Celesta one last time. "I'm sure. You are free to do whatever you want."

"May the wind be with you," Celesta said.

Zidika got of his unicorn. He removed the saddles from both unicorns and threw them on the ground. Both the unicorns ran happily into the fields, and Rena and Zidika watched them run off into the sunset. Beautiful pink and orange colors where painted though out the whole sky.

"Those unicorns were pretty fast," said Zidika. "They got us close to our destination within a day. A regular horse would have taken at least three days and three nights."

"Yes, these unicorns are pretty fast." Then Rena felt guilt taking over. She looked at Zidika and frowned.

Zidika noticed right away. "What is it?" he said coming closer.

"I'm sorry, Zidika, for not telling you this sooner."

"Telling me what sooner?"

"Remember that time when you lost me at the beach? Well, I was actually trapped in a cave. When I escaped, I met a girl named Rin. She asked me for a favor."

"What was the favor?" Zidika looked as if he did not mind.

"She asked me to rescue her friend from her captives."

"What?"

"I'm sorry I didn't tell you this sooner."

"I'm not mad about that. It's just that you're willing to rescue some girl you don't know anything about and willing to sacrifice our whole mission."

"It's just the same as rescuing my brother. Besides, they live in the same place we are going to. Maybe I can just find her and bring her back home."

"Do whatever you want. It's your mission." He paused, looking at Rena. "Let's camp in that cave over there," said Zidika pointing to a huge cave. They both walked into it and laid down their stuff. Rena sat down, but not beside Zidika. She made sure to keep her distance. "In the morning, we'll find the cave of the dragons," Rena said looking at the Zidika.

"Yes. Now get some sleep."

Rena lay down closing her eyes. Not many minutes had passed before Rena suddenly woke up. She wasn't able to sleep because a certain thought was stuck in her head. She sat up and noticed that Zidika wasn't sleeping. "Zidika," she said softly.

Zidika turned to face her. "Yes, what is it? Why aren't you sleeping?" he asked.

Rena tried to sound confident in what she was about to say. "What do you think about Sara?" That question suddenly amazed him, and Rena felt as if Sara had all of a sudden awakened inside of her. "Please, I just want to know what you think about her. What is your relationship?" A red blush appeared on her face, and she didn't look directly at Zidika because of her embarrassment. Rena felt that Sara wanted to say something, but Rena held her breath and didn't say a word. Rena saw the gleam in his eyes. That was what she was afraid of. It wasn't that she had something against Sara. It was that Sara didn't really exist anymore. She felt that Zidika had to move on from Sara and find another girl—a girl who would care for him. She was hoping it would be her.

"What is there to say?"

Rena had not expected that from him. She thought that he would start talking about her nonstop. Was he teasing her? Was he trying to find her limits until she would erupt in a hurricane of yelling? Was he doing this on purpose, just to get her angry? Her head started spinning around in circles. She couldn't take this anymore. She needed to know. It was not as if he had told her that he loved Sara. The answer then might have already been given to her. But she needed to know what he thought of Sara, and maybe, just maybe, from his answer, she would be able to move on and never again be glued to one guy. Finally she might be able to unstick herself. "Why are you doing this to me, Zidika? Don't you understand what I'm feeling right now? This is so hard for me. I need to know, and you're not making things any better for me."

Zidika suddenly looked at her with eyes that reflected the fact that he was sorry for what he had done, but the truth was he didn't know what he had done to make her so upset. "I'm sorry, Rena, if I may have upset you. But can you tell me why knowing what I thought about Sara could make you so upset?"

"You still don't understand it." Her big brown eyes widened in sadness and anger. "This is just so hard for me. I don't know what to think. I just want to know." She begged and pleaded until he looked at her a little coldly.

"I used to love her." A cold air blew into the cave and froze everything around it. Everything was standing still; everything froze. Rena felt as if her heart had fallen all the way to her feet. *Used to?* she thought. *What does he mean by that? Does that mean he has gotten over her? Has he moved on? Does he have feelings for another? If so who is she?*

The cave was suddenly hot—burning hot as if there was a fire in the cave. Was it just her or was the cave really that hot? She looked around and saw no fire. So it was just her. She was feeling hot all of a sudden. "Zidika, do you feel how hot it is?"

Zidika leaned close to Rena, but he was not looking at her. His eyes widened as he stared at the thing behind her. "Rena." He spoke quietly.

"Yes, Zidika?"

"There is a dragon behind you." Rena did not understand at first. She looked at him in a confused way. "Rena, get out of here. There is a dragon behind you." Rena finally understood. She wanted to scream, but Zidika stopped her. "No sudden movements, no loud noises."

Then the dragon spoke to them. "What brings you here? Why have you come to my cave?" he asked. His voice was monstrous; it caused the inside of the cave to tremble.

"We have come here to ask for your help." Zidika spoke in as calming a voice as he could manage.

"Help? And what makes you think that you're worthy of my help?"

"Rena, on the count of three we run. Get it?" Zidikia whispered in her ear. "One … two … three …*run!*" Zidika got up and lunged for the mouth of the cave. Rena stood up as quickly as she could. She grabbed her backpack from the floor, and just as she was about to run, the orb rolled out of the pack. Rena stared at the orb, and soon her eyes turned completely red—a solid red. She lost all control, and lost all connection with Sara. She walked over to the orb and picked it up. Holding it out in front of her, she walked toward the dragon.

The dragon breathed fire in all directions, warning Rena not to come close. "I will burn you alive!" he said. No matter what was blown at her, Rena continued to walk forward. "Stop, girl! Stop right there!" But the dragon's warning did not work, so he breathed fire right at her. The orb suddenly cast a crystal-like red bubble around Rena that deflected the fire. The dragon's flame blew to Rena's right and burned a piece of rock.

Even the dragon could not stop Rena until she reached what she was supposed to get—a white stone attached to the end of a stick. The twigs of the stick formed a spherical cage that protected the stone from any harm. Rena walked up to the stone and released it from its protector. Once she did, she regained consciousness and began to fall to the ground. The dragon caught her with its talc.

"This girl!" The dragon looked at the orb on the ground.

Zidika looked into the cave. He was worried because Rena had not come out. He couldn't believe that he saw Rena lying on the dragon's tail. He walked over the dragon, again speechless. *How is she able to do all this? Is it because of the orb that is lying on the ground?*

"She has earned my loyalty," whispered the dragon.

CHAPTER 16

Kiche, Dragon of the Sky

• •

Rena woke up and felt a cool breeze bite her skin. She couldn't remember what had happened. She freaked when she saw a scaly tail and realized she was sitting on it. "What's going on here?" And to her surprise, when she looked up, she saw the dragon sleeping. "Zidika! Zidika!" she yelled, and that caused the dragon to wake up. It moved its tail just a little, which startled Rena, so she jumped off. Then she saw Zidika. She ran up to him. "Zidika, what's going on? Why was I sleeping on the dragon's tail? Why isn't he trying to burn us?" she asked. A million more questions buzzed in her head. Panic took over, and she could hardly breathe.

"Rena, calm down." He paused. "We won. Whatever you did proved to the dragon that we are worthy. We will now have his full cooperation. How are you able to do all these things?"

Rena looked down at the orb. All she could remember about what happened was that the orb had rolled out of her pack. No, she couldn't believe it was all because of this orb. "All I did was take this stone," she said, holding it up.

"That stone was part of my test," said the dragon. "I was testing you to see if you were able to get it from me. I was testing you to see if you would be afraid." He turned to Zidika. "With this girl's courage, you could go through a lot of things. Keep that in mind." He turned back to Rena.

"Never lose your faith or your courage. You will always need it wherever life takes you."

Rena turned around and looked at the dragon now that he was so close to her. She smiled, trying not to show that she was a little scared. He seemed about a hundred feet taller than she would have imaged a dragon to be.

"Sorry if I frightened you," said the dragon. "I know you are a bit scared of me, but I can assure you that I won't harm you."

Rena smiled a bit more. She looked at the stone in her hand and held it out to the dragon. "Here you go. I bet you want it back."

"Keep it. That stone has special property, and I entrust you with its care. You were brave enough to overcome your fear."

"Actually, I don't remember what happened," Rena admitted. "It was almost as if I was not myself, but rather someone else."

Then Zidika remembered. He was the only one who had seen her eyes turning red. When he saw that, he could tell that something was wrong. But it didn't matter now. Because of what had happened to her, they had earned the dragon's trust.

"I am Kiche, the sky dragon. There are four of us dragons remaining in this world. I can breathe out both air and fire. I am your guide to wherever you need to go. I am your servant till the very end."

"No, we don't want you to be out servant," said Rena. "We just want you to be our friend. Count yourself as part of the group, and don't think yourself as any less." She smiled brightly at the beast.

Those words made him feel so warm inside. "Thank you, miss."

"Call me Rena."

"Rena, you're one of the oddest people I have ever come across. I see that you have changed a lot since you came here."

Rena smiled a little. "You're right. I have changed. I don't usually act like this with other people. I don't know why, but for some odd reason this place makes me feel different. All the people and creatures I have met, and what I have seen, have made an impression on me that has changed me." She smiled as she remembered her experiences. Then she pushed all the thoughts back into her head.

Then again, she looked at the red orb, which still lay next to the dragon. She walked up to it and took it into her hands. Her eyes turned a little red as she stared at the ball and held it out. Zidika walked up to her. "Maybe it would be better if I take this," he said taking it from her hands. He put it back into her backpack.

"That orb," said Kiche. "You were holding it out just as you did then. You showed no emotion as you walked forward. This orb gives me a strange feeling, and I don't like it."

After a few minutes, Rena got down to business. "Have you ever heard of a land in the west of Nippon?"

"Yes, I have. And I can tell you that it is one of the most dangerous places in the entire world. Why would you want to go there?"

"Well, you see, my little brother was possessed by a centipede and kidnapped. I was told that I would be able to find him there. Plus, I made a promise to a friend." She looked a Zidika, who was rolling his eyes at her last words. Rena ignored him.

"You say a centipede?"

"Yes, do you know anything about it?"

"Yes, I do. There is only one centipede I can think of. Its name is Mukade, and he is a symbol of evil. He is one of the most ruthless and dangerous creatures you ever want to face. Even if you just see this creature, it's most likely that you will be scarred for life. It is a pity that your brother was possessed by it. It's likely that you will never see him again. Why would he possess a young child instead of just killing the boy right away?"

"Well, you see, I have something inside of me that the demon wants."

"Huh. He wants to bargain with you?

"Well, something like that, but you see, this thing that he wants is in me, and it would cost me my life to give it to him, so I'm trying to find a way to get my brother back without any bargaining."

"Well, Rena," said Kiche, "that would be extremely difficult to do. You must plan out everything. You must know what to do. Do you even know what you're going to do when you find him?"

"I'm focusing all of my strength on finding him first."

"Rena, you're a strong-willed girl, and if anyone can defeat him, I believe it could be you. But I am worried that the demon might be too strong, defeating it might take a lot of effort

Rena smiled at him almost evilly. "I've got it all under control. Now let's get going."

Kiche the dragon knelt down in front of them and let Zidika and Rena get on his back. He flew out with such a great force that Rena felt the sky was trembling. She fell back as she tried to hold on with all her strength. The dragon made twists and loops as he suddenly flew forward. Kiche was probably enjoying this as much as Rena and Zidika were. They flew past villages and watched as people looked at them from below. It felt nice.

Zidika suddenly felt as if wanted to get close to Rena. Back in the cave she had suddenly been acting weird, wanting to know what he thought about Sara. He liked that about her. He sensed that she was jealous. Back in the cave, he had wanted to hold her tightly and tell her how much she meant to him. Now was the most perfect time to get near her. She looked so happy, beautiful, and charming. He felt that she wouldn't mind him holding her.

As Kiche suddenly flew sharply up into the air, Rena was thrown backward. She tumbled over and soon found herself in the arms of Zidika. They both turned red as Rena quickly sat up. She sat still for a second, and then she looked over at Zidika. He was staring at her and wouldn't look away. What was he doing? Why was he acting like this? Why was he staring at her and only her? She saw her reflection in his eyes and saw the blue sky behind her. Rena acted as if she didn't notice and turned away. She blushed even more. She felt her heart racing.

She smiled to herself as she remembered that smile he had given her before, when he was laughing. It was the pure smile of joy and happiness. When he laughed at her, she felt embarrassed, but she also felt happy. Why would she feel happy? Why did she want to be happy? She was the kind of girl who didn't care, but now she was starting to care. Now she knew. She was different now; she was not her old self anymore. She was a changed person; she had released the person who had been locked up inside of her for three years. Three years. That's how long Zidika had said he'd been in that place. Could he have something to do with her? Three years … three years … three years. What could that mean? Huh. It didn't matter, it was probably coincidence.

She knew now that she was thankful. She should enjoy her life because everything that she loved could be taken away from her in an instant. For that reason, she had to enjoy every single little thing that came into her life. Her life could change so much; she might never live the same life again. Just as she had told Rin, she did not have to be afraid, she didn't have to lock herself up in a cage as Rin had done just to escape from the world. *Rin was too afraid*, thought Rena. *Afraid to open herself again, to see to the world. Maybe she was afraid that she was going to get hurt again. In life, there are a lot of things we have to do that we don't like, but we do them because we have to. I should live my life to the fullest and then leave this life with no regrets. I'm not going to stay young forever. I'd better start living before I'm sixty. I don't want to be kicking myself for the rest of my life asking myself why I didn't do this or that.*

Rena turned to look a Zidika. She saw the passion in his eyes. He had been alone for so long that he needed somebody without knowing that he did. He pushed people away when what he really wanted was some company, someone to talk to. He moved slowly toward Rena. He placed a kiss on her lips. She let him.

CHAPTER 17

The First

• • • • • • • • • • •

They flew for days without stopping. The wind danced around them. It was dark now. Rena slept near Zidika, his arm around her. Kiche flew past another village and slowly diminished his speed. Rena's hair stopped flying and was pushed back down around her shoulders. Kiche hovered above a tree filled with rich fruits. He knew the fruit was juicy and as sweet as honey. He landed near the tree.

Rena woke up. She noticed Zidika near her and was happy to see him. She didn't mind him being near her because she knew his answer to her questions. She sat up. "What is it?" she said in a sleepy voice as she rubbed her eyes.

"You haven't eaten for a few days," said Kiche. "It would be good for you to stock up on some of these fruits." For some reason Rena did not feel hungry. She looked over at Zidika, who was still sleeping. She smiled and slid off Kiche's back. She looked back at Zidika and thought about the feeling he gave her. It was like an addiction to sweet chocolate. It didn't matter to her that they hadn't eaten for a few days, as long as she could fall asleep under his protection.

She thought of picking up some of the fruits that had fallen onto the ground, but then thought that the most delicious ones would still be up in the trees. Rena set down her pack and started to climb the tree. She had always hated heights, but now, since the ride on Kiche, she no longer felt scared or worried. And that dangerous climb up the cliff in the cave had really helped her a lot as well. She now knew what branches would be best to step on. She was happy that she could still be like a child. She almost laughed as she remembered her childhood friends climbing trees to pick fruits and getting yelled at by their parents or the neighbors because they were in trees that didn't belong to them.

She got high enough into the tree that she could reach one of the fruits. She pulled it from the branch and bit into it. She felt as if a party had exploded in her mouth. All the rich juices were so sweet! She felt as if she was fruit from heaven. The rich, sweet juices tasted like honey. Rena picked a few more from the tree, dropping them onto the ground. She climbed down from the tree and picked up her prizes, making sure none were bruised.

As she opened her pack to put the fruits in, she noticed the flowers she had taken off the unicorn. They were red, the color of blood. And they were still fresh and smelled delightful, as if they had just been picked that morning. Then her gaze fell to the orb. She didn't feel anything different this time; she did not black out as she had done before. Why was that? What was that? Before, whenever she touched the orb or even just glanced at it, she had blacked out and lost consciousness. She had been separated from her body. She hadn't felt like herself anymore. It was as if the orb had taken possession of her, as if someone else had taken control of her the way Sara had done several times. Rena had become a different person every time she looked at the orb. Every time it took hold of her spirit, she had lost control and parted from herself. She was afraid that, over time, it could take control of her permanently. Zidika was the only one who had been able to help her break loose. He was the only one who could help her, and would help her. She knew that and trusted him.

She felt great energy coming from the orb—great, powerful evil energy. It consumed her body and soul a little bit every time she encountered it. Then why hadn't she gotten rid of it? Why did she still keep it, even though she knew it meant no good? She thought it would come in handy. She thought she might need it for the great battle that was about to come.

"Rena, that orb. Let me see it." Sara was back.

"I'm sorry, Sara. I can't do that. If I do, something terrible might happen. It is best if I keep it hidden and away from my sight."

"Perhaps you are right," agreed Sara. "Every time you glanced at it, you lost control, and I lost all contact with you. It was as if something had possessed your body, taken it over. I felt a great, powerful presence … something evil. Why do you still keep that orb?"

"It might help. It might come in handy." Rena pulled out the flowers from the pack. She looked at them for a couple of seconds and then, just as she was going to drop them onto the floor, thorns appeared on the stems, and one of them pricked her finger. Blood ran out of Rena's wound and fell onto the roses, mixing with the color. Then the blood dripped from the roses, and a few drops of blood fell onto the orb. Rena covered up her finger as she felt the pain. Her finger felt as if it had been burned. This was all very weird because there had been no thorns on the garland of flowers before. The blood went into the orb. It mixed in with the colors in the orb and soon became a part of it.

Suddenly a heavy wind blew. It sent Rena flying into Kiche. But then it lifted her up. She floated in the air. Soon she blacked out. Her eyes turned blank; there was no color. But this was not like the blackouts she'd experienced before. This time she saw something—a vision. Deep inside a forest, in a snowy cave, she saw an ice sculpture. And inside the ice sculpture was a body. Sara's body. She hadn't aged, hadn't been touched by time. The wind set Rena down onto the ground gently, and she soon regained consciousness.

"Sara," Rena said. "I saw something that might make you very happy."

"What is it?" answered Sara. "Is it how to get your brother back?"

"Something better."

"What? Tell me!" She almost sounded excited.

"I saw how to get your body back."

Sara did not speak, and Rena could tell that she was shocked, but not in a good way. Sara remained silent, and then she spoke in a serious tone. "How do you know about that? No one is supposed to know about it. I sealed it off so no one could ever get to it or know about it. How is it that you suddenly know?"

"But I thought you would be happy to hear it."

"No, I'm not."

"But why? Aren't you happy? Soon you will have your own body and you won't have to share with me. Why aren't you happy about this?"

"Because it's not good. I separated from my body for a reason, and if someone knows about it, it can't be good."

But Rena did not listen to Sara. Rena started walking to Kiche. She climbed onto him. Zidika was still sleeping. She told Kiche to change direction and go the opposite way from the way they had been traveling.

"What are you doing?" Sara asked. "Don't you want to save your brother?"

"I'm going to find your body."

"Rena, you can't!"

"Watch me," Rena said in a darkened voice. She no longer behaved like herself.

Zidika had awakened. He saw that Rena was awake. She was sitting far from him, close to the dragon's head. She looked different. She had changed. This was not Rena. This was not her.

It got dark by the time Kiche reached the forest. "Rena, you've got to listen to me," Sara pleaded. "Turn back before it's too late."

"Oh, how pathetic," croaked Rena. "The almighty Sara, of whom everyone speaks so highly, and with whom Zidika has fallen in love. You can't even use your powers to stop me." Rena slid off Kiche. Her face darkened as she started walking.

Zidika couldn't believe that it was Rena who had just spoken. But what she had said wasn't all a lie. He used to have feelings for Sara. But those feeling had changed when he met Rena. She gave him different feelings— feelings he had never felt before, feelings that he never had for Sara. Rena was everything to him. But the girl who stood before him now was not his Rena.

Rena walked as Zidika followed her. She didn't even stop once while Zidika tripped and stumbled over tree branches and roots. She was determined to reach her destination. It became colder as Rena went deeper into the forest. The icy wind pinched and bit at her skin, but she did not even flinch from the cold. Soon the forest turned to ice. Snow covered everything. Zidika looked around in amazement, but Rena kept on walking. The cold got to Zidika, and soon he started shivering. She didn't even stop for a second. Her speed increased as they came closer to a cave.

Rena smiled evilly as she walked into the cave. There, at the far end, stood an ice sculpture that encased a person's body. "I have found it," she said. But her voice didn't sound like her own.

"Rena, stop please," said Sara.

"Why should I do that when I'm so close?"

"Who is speaking?" Sara had finally realized that it was not Rena.

Rena did not answer. Instead, she walked up to the huge ice sculpture. She summoned her terrifying fire power, the same one she had used on the girl back at the village. The lightning bolt struck the ice and soon engulfed it, turning into a black kind of fire that ate away the ice. When the ice was completely gone. Rena used her snow power to make sure that nothing would happen to the body.

Sara's body fell forward, but Rena caught it and placed it gently on the ground. "Finally," she said. She traced finger around Sara's cheek, feeling the softness of her skin.

"Why have you possessed Rena's body?" Sara asked. "Who are you?"

"You will soon find out," said the unknown entity. Sara tried to use her powers to take over Rena's body again, but she was too weak. Whoever was possessing Rena's body was too powerful. Not even Sara could do anything about it.

Rena traced a star in the air with her finger. When she finished, it glowed bright purple. A symbol appeared inside the star. Rena's hands started moving in a rhythmic pattern as they had back in the village. She started making more symbols in the air with her hands. She spoke in several different languages, and in several different voices. Soon she created her last symbol in the air. She then placed her hand on Sara's stomach. The star vanished from the air and soon appeared on Sara's stomach.

A strong breeze blew, pushing everything out of the way. Sara's hair lifted above her head, but soon fell back down. She had awakened from a long slumber. She was here against her will. She had always known what would happen if she ever returned to her body. Her soul returned, and she felt her heart beat. Her eyes opened, and she saw someone in front of her, a person of evil. An evil presence surrounded her. It came from within Rena. The evil escaped from Rena, and Rena fell forward, but before she reached the ground, Zidika caught her and placed her down gently on the ground, his hands holding hers. He looked at Sara and then at the evil presence that filled the cave. "Who are you? What do you want with us? Why have you possessed Rena?" he shouted.

"I haven't entirely possessed her," said the voice. "She could have stopped me if she wanted to. She's that powerful. But no, she came here because of her simple will."

"Aegleca, can it be you?" Sara said sitting up.

"It's been a long time."

"So, it is you." Sara stood up. The expression on her face was unreadable.

"For too long I have been trapped in that orb," said Aegleca. "Now I have escaped!"

"You were supposed to be banished forever," said Sara. "How is it that you were still able to possess this girl? How is it that you could be set free by returning me to my body? I knew this couldn't be good, but this is far from good."

"It was all this girl. You don't give her enough credit, Sara. She is powerful—more powerful than you could even imagine. I was able to take control of her little by little. She may have been powerful, but does have a weak and venerable spot. It stems from the death of her father and then what happened to her mother and her brother. Her heart was in pain, and it was easy for me to take control of her."

Zidika looked at Rena, who was still in his arms and still unconscious. He quickly pulled the orb from her bag and looked at it. The color was no longer there. Nothing swirled around inside it. It was as white as snow.

"What happened?" demanded Sara, walking up to Aegleca. "Why did you change so many years ago? Why did you pick the wrong path? You have caused everyone so much pain, and all for what?" His face was as hard as stone. He showed no emotion. She saw anger only in his eyes. "Together we could have done a lot of good," she said. "Why did you choose the wrong path?"

His eyes softened a little but only for a short time. "Because I am a demon. I cannot be human; neither can I try to be a human."

"But you didn't act like a demon. I saw you as a human not a beast. What changed your mind?"

"Enough!" He looked at Rena. Lifting his hand, he took hold of Rena, and she was brought to him.

"This girl may never wake," he told both of them. "She will remain trapped in her own world where everything seems real but isn't, where she will have to choose from reality or a dream."

Sara looked at Rena. She wanted to do something to save her, but she knew she had no chance against Aegleca. He was too powerful for her.

"If she doesn't wake up in twenty-four hours, her power will be mine," announced Aegleca.

"No!" Zidika shouted. "You can't take her away!" Why was it like this? What was it all about? Why was everything he cared about taken away? They say that the reason people feel lonely it is that they have experienced happiness and joy, and then it's all taken away. This time it wasn't going to be like that. He was not going to let it happen—not again. He was going to do whatever it took in his power to save her. But it would take more than his power alone. He could save her only if she let him, only if she wanted to be saved.

He ripped off the only thing that kept his powers in check. His blood grew cold. His eyes turned blood red. A bright red light shot up from him and into the sky and crumbled into pieces as it revealed the dark-blue night sky. The blue light of the bright and beautiful moon slowly began to change color. The baby-blue color of the moon became darker, and it soon turned completely red.

Sara stared at the moon and then at Zidika, not believing that he was a ckii tsuki. He had been one of them this whole time, and she had never known. She looked at the ground and saw the thing he had ripped off his neck. It seemed to have kept his powers in check. She walked over to it and picked it up. It was a golden locket. It opened so that the wearer could keep a picture inside, but Sara found nothing inside. She looked back up at Zidika. She had to stop him.

Running toward him, Sara pulled out her sword. Since she had her body back, her old powers had returned. She ran in front of Zidika before he completely started destroying things. She knew how great the power he possessed was. "Zidika, this is not the way things are supposed to be."

"Get out of my way!"

"No! Believe me, I want to rescue Rena as much as you do, but not like this."

"Get out or I will kill you."

"I don't think this is the time you guys should be fighting against each other," said Aegleca. "Come to me when you both are ready." With that said, he was gone.

Zidika lunged forward to stop him, but Sara stopped Zidika. "Whose side are you on?" he yelled.

She made a blue orb with her hands and encircled both of them with it to keep them from leaving. "This is not the right time or place to be doing this," she said. "Look, do you want to be yourself to save Rena? You can't always be depending on your powers to do the work for you. One day they will be gone, and you will be stuck because all you did was depend on something other than yourself to get you through, and you won't know how to deal with it by yourself."

Zidika's eyes turned back to their original color. He fell to the ground. The orb around them disappeared. "Then what am I supposed to do?"

Sara came up to him. She took him into her arms. Zidika had tears in his eyes. The cave around them started crumbling down. "We should get out," Sara said sweetly. Zidika stood up. He and Sara walked out of the cave as it crumbled behind them. "Zidika, I can assure you that I would do anything in my power to bring her back."

"We need to think of something," said Zidika. "We can't just go in there without at least a plan."

Sara smiled as they walked to Kiche. She hadn't felt this way in a long time. She hadn't had these feelings. She thought she had forgotten the feelings.

CHAPTER 18

Dream or Reality

. . . .

When Aegleca stepped into his castle, everything sprang to life. Thorns and weeds that had grown through the cracks in the floors disappeared. Green moss vanished from the walls and ceilings. Red roses bloomed everywhere, thick with thorns. Everything returned to the way it had been before. Just twenty-four hours, and then Rena would be his. Twenty-four hours, and he could have his revenge.

"Where am I?" Rena asked. "What am I doing here?" She looked at the reflection of her family, and then she suddenly was with her family—her father and mother, her brother, her grandparents, and even her childhood friends. All were sitting at the kitchen table enjoying each other's company. What was this? Was this a dream? She would have known if this was a dream. She knew the difference between dream and reality. But this illusion seemed so real. It was an illusion, wasn't it? She looked at the people sitting at the table. They laughed and talked as they passed food around. They were just having a normal conversation the way they would every Sunday.

"Why am I here? Why is Dad here? Why is Joey here? If they are all here, that means it all must have been a dream. Dad's death, mother in a modeling career, Joey getting kidnapped and brought to a different world, and me changing my personality and traveling to a different world in order to rescue Joey. Then it all must have been a dream. That means I never met Zidika." Somehow she felt the loneliness in her heart. It was as if she was forgetting something, a part of her life, as if something was missing. So this wasn't an illusion, but the real thing. She must have dreamed it all, the other part of her life. Then the laughter of everyone brought her back, and she just sat happily with them, laughing with them, enjoying her life.

"It must have been a dream. All of it was a dream." She smiled at her parents, and they smiled back at her. After a while, Rena felt lonely. She longed for something to fill that loneliness. Nothing she did filled that void in her heart. Yet, when she was dreaming, when everything seemed and felt so real, she felt happy, as if her life was full, as if that was where she belonged and nowhere else but there.

Ding, ding, ding. Her clock rang. It was time for school. Rena got up, got ready, and headed out. Her friends met up with her, and they all started heading for school. As they were leaving, Rena turned back and looked at their house. It might have been a little small, but it was cozy. It had its own charm. *Yet something doesn't seem right*, she thought. *It is as if this is not a dream. Instead it is as if I have forgotten something important.*

"Rena, come back to us," said Achila, one of her childhood friends, a girl with short blue hair and thin eyebrows. "Were you daydreaming again?"

Rena looked at her and smiled. "Yeah, that's all." Yet she still felt as if something was missing, as if something was wrong.

CHAPTER 19

Snow Maiden

• • • • • • • • • • • • •

"We have only three more hours left," Zidika told Sara as they headed back to the tree with the mouthwatering fruits. "What are we going to do?"

"We are going to get help," Sara said.

"From who?"

"The outsiders."

"Who?"

"People who have awakened their powers but don't know what for," said Sara. "And they have been cast away from their hometowns. We are going to find them and get their help."

"Will we save Rena in time?"

"Don't have doubt in your heart, son," said Sara.

"Explain something to me," said Zidika. "How is it that the demon could have possessed Rena if she is so powerful? Why did you talk to him in such a warm voice, as if you knew him? How is it that such a powerful centipede can be possessed by this demon?"

"You ask too many questions."

"Questions that I want answers to. Now tell me."

"As you heard," said Sara, "the demon was able to possess Rena—take hold of her—because she had a weak heart. She was afraid. She wasn't strong enough to destroy her own demon, which lurked deep within her heart." Zidika remembered all those times he had seen Rena cry, and he felt bad. "The reason I talked to him like that," Sara continued, "was that I knew him long ago. I came across a flower patch in which tall grass and all different kinds of brightly colored flowers grew. That was when I saw him lying in the tall grass. He had a piece of grass in his mouth, and he was lying with his hands behind his head. He was sleeping. I was fascinated by him. I fell in love with him right there and then. When he woke, he saw me and fell in love. We both shared that place; it was our secret, and we used to meet there in private. But some people of my village followed me when they saw me leaving too many times. They saw me meeting with the demon. They told me I would never see him again. I had to do what my village people wanted me to do. And so that very last day we spent together was his last and my very last. I told him that I couldn't see him anymore. At first, he was disappointed and asked me why. But when I couldn't give him a good enough reason, his demon blood came out. He turned into the creature he had tried so hard to hold back—a human-like, but with only half a face. He threatened to destroy my village, and I couldn't let that happen, so I used my sealing powers to seal the demon off and put him into an orb. I was just so young back then that I didn't know what I was doing."

Sara looked down at her hands. Zidika looked at her, and he could see that she was very upset. She still loved Aegleca. No matter what he did, she couldn't tear him from her heart. It killed her inside seeing the one she loved hurting others because of her. Then Sara looked back up at Zidika. "As to your final question, the demon Mukade—the centipede—is truly a powerful demon. Many demons fear it, but that doesn't mean that there won't be some other demons that turn out to be more powerful than it is. It is hard to believe that he could have possessed such a powerful demon when he was in the orb, but that just proves that he is that much stronger.

The only way that you can travel though the mirror and get back to the other world, if you are from that world—" Then she stopped herself. "You knew that Rena wasn't from this world."

Zidika smiled. "Of course. Her strange clothes, the way she spoke, her attitude, her personality."

"Then you must also—" she said this as if she had just realized something very important, but before she could finish her sentence, Zidika interrupted."Go on, finish," he said.

"Right. But if the creature isn't from the other world, then that would mean that the person must have something that belonged from that world. It must have that thing in order to travel to the other side." Then Sara remembered something. "Zidika, that necklace you have around your neck. It is supposed to have a picture in it, right?"

"Yes," Zidika said, taking it off. "It's a picture of my mother and me." When he opened it to show her, shock overtook him because the locket was empty. "What? Where is the picture? No! I can't believe I lost it. It was the only thing I had left to remind me of my parents." He was very angry. "That's right. The picture must have fallen out, and that is how the centipede traveled to the other world." But Zidika was too upset to even think.

Suddenly the air grew colder and white puffs of snow began to fall from the sky. Soon the whole area around them was completely covered in snow. A little storm was underway. Kiche landed on the snow near a frozen waterfall. Sara and Zidika slid off, and Sara told Kicke, "Wait, please. We will be back soon." She gently kissed the dragon's cheek. "Thank you for everything you have done, Kiche."

"Come, Sara," said Zidika. "We do not have much time. Only two hours and thirty minutes left." The wind blew harder as they walked farther and farther into the blizzard. The snow completely covered them by the time they stumbled upon bricks made out of ice. Sara said, "This is the Snow Queen's castle. This is where she finds all of the girls who have ice powers. She brings them here. She doesn't harm them; she just trains them so they get used to their powers and are not frightened by them. She does not allow men here."

"Then how will I get inside?"

Sara faced him and looked at him in a mischievous way. "This is where my favorite part comes." In a few minutes Sara knocked on the castle wall. "Hello!" she hollered. "I have come here to see the Snow Queen. Let us pass." The gate opened, and Sara and Zidika entered. They saw girls of all ages training with long spears. Some looked to be around fifteen, and some appeared to be even younger, perhaps twelve. They all wore the same kind of clothing—plain white wool trimmed in animal fur. They all had red ribbons tied to their ankles, and they all wore their hair pulled back. They wore headbands on their foreheads as well.

When they saw Sara and Zidika enter, they acted as if they had never seen outsiders before. But they were excited to see these beautiful girls walking by. One had long, beautiful, shimmering red hair, and the other had short white hair that curled at the tips and bounced around whenever she took a step. They were both tall and beautiful with angelic faces, pale skin, rosy pink cheeks, and red lipstick. They both walked gracefully. The one with the white hair wore a fur coat, and the other one wore a plain cloth jacket. The girls started staring and then followed them.

Zidika started worrying that maybe they had seen through his disguise. They walked up toward the most beautiful woman of them all—fair lady with white skin, as if it had been painted by the snow. Her apple cheeks were painted with dark red blush, and her eyes were crystal blue. She wore a fur jacket, and her hair was neatly tied into a bun with a ribbon. When they approached her, they bowed down before the woman started to speak. "Who honors us with a visit?" she asked.

"I am Sara, and this is my closest friend, Cherika. We have come here to ask for your help, if you would be so kind as to willingly lend us your hand in this battle we are facing."

The queen stood up from her seat. "Sara, we are old friends. Why do you approach me like this? I am honored to have such a powerful spiritual woman come here, asking for my help. It is an honor. Whatever you need I shall give you."

"We ask to use your girls in a battle. If you like, you may come with us as well."

"Why would you need to use my girls?"

"A dear friend of mine had been captured by Aegleca. You may have heard that name. But my friend happens to be more powerful than he is. He is planning to use her power along with his own. Their powers combined not only will cause great destruction to our world, but to both worlds. It will be the end for all of us. But he doesn't realize that. He is so focused on his revenge that he doesn't see what he may do."

"And how do you suppose he will obtain her power if she is more powerful than he is?"

"Her heart was weak, and she allowed herself to be possessed by this demon. After he captured her, he put her under a reality spell in which she believed she had escaped into her own world where everything isn't real. She has twenty-four hours to wake up or he will take control of her. We don't have much time."

"I see what you mean, but I cannot put my girls' lives in danger. Some have been training with me for a long time, but some have just begun. I cannot do this to them. Their winter power may not be strong enough."

"I understand," said Sara.

Disappointed, Sara turned to leave, but just then, one of the girls spoke up—a tiny girl with black pigtails. "We want to help." All the girls looked at her and agreed.

"Fine," said the queen. "But be careful. I trust you will come home safely."

"Yes," they all said in one voice. The gate opened and all the girls marched out. They took their spears with them, holding them tightly as they walked. The winter cold did not seem to bother them at all. It was as if they were used to it, or it felt like summer to them.

When they finally reached Kiche, there were only ninety minutes left. "Do you think we can make it in time?" Zidika asked.

"I don't know," said Sara. "All this weight could cause Kiche to slow down. We can't afford to lose any time."

"Perhaps we can help," said a familiar voice that she knew too well. All the girls turned around to see Celesta. With her were many more unicorns, many of them carrying female riders. Sara felt overjoyed when she saw them.

All the unicorns stood together neighing and talking with each other. The girls who sat on them seemed to be from the water and fire nation. Some of them had weapons with them, and some didn't. They all talked with each other.

Zidika couldn't believe it. He had never seen such a big herd in one place. Everyone wanted to help. They wanted to save Rena. It made him so happy, he felt like crying.

"I had a vision that Rena would soon be in trouble," said Celesta. "And I had to repay her for her kindness. So, as soon as I started on my journey here, I searched for many more unicorns who could help. I also encountered the remaining tribes of girls like them, but with water and fire powers. Unfortunately, I couldn't find any who could turn the moon red."

"That doesn't really matter," said Sara. "You have done enough already. Thank you so much."

"I know Rena is a special girl," said Celesta. "She is destined to do great things." Sara nodded. Then she got down to business. "I need thirty girls with me to ride on the dragon. The rest of you, find a unicorn that doesn't have a rider and follow us."

Celesta walked over to Kiche. "It's been a long time," the dragon said, trying to sound friendly.

But Celesta knew he was trying his best, and she smiled. "Sorry," Celesta said. Kiche looked at her. He had not expected an apology. "Sorry for what we did in the past, for what our ancestors did to your kind. But that was all in the past, so can we just forget this and try to save the one person who matters to both of us?"

Kiche smiled. "Okay then, let's go!" And he flew up into the air. Celesta and her herd made a shining light with their horns and ran after Kiche with great speed.

CHAPTER 20

This Isn't Reality

· ·

I'*m happy here, and I don't ever want to leave*, Rena thought, as she walked home from school with her childhood friends. She felt something in her pocket. It felt like a stone. She pulled it out and stopped walking as she stared at it. Her friends didn't seem to notice and kept walking, laughing and talking among themselves.

What is this? Rena thought. The stone was crystal white. It had a smooth surface, and it was shaped like an egg. The stone glowed and let out a surprising bright light that circled around her and then showed her an image. Three girls surrounded her in this image. They were laughing, and she was laughing with them. They did not look like the childhood friends she had just been walking with. *Who are these girls and why am I laughing with them? Why do I look so happy?* She felt something in her heart, as if something had filled a small part of the loneliness she had been feeling. The image disappeared. Rena saw that her childhood friends had left her all alone. Then the stone showed her another image. In this image, she was at her dad's funeral. Her family members were all wearing black and they all were crying. "This is Dad's funeral," Rena said as she covered her mouth. Tears appeared in her eyes as she remembered that day. The image went away, and soon another one appeared. This image was her mom at her photo shoot. "This is Mom's new job," she said, looking at the image until it vanished. She almost remembered it. Another image came—her brother being taken away. This image lasted longer than the rest. She saw herself entering the alternate world and meeting Zidika. She saw all of their adventures. Rena smiled a bit as she remembered. This information filled the loneliness in her heart. This was what she had been seeking all along. This place—the place she had been thinking was home—this wasn't real. This was all a dream. She missed Zidika. She wanted to see him. This wasn't reality, but a dream. She wanted to see Zidika, she wanted to see everyone.

***

"We have fifty minutes left," Zidika told Sara.

The snow girls who were riding with them looked a Zidika in a strange way. Zidika looked at them, and then remembered that he hadn't taken off the wig. "So, you were a boy this whole time?" one of the girls said in amazement.

"Yeah."

"You looked pretty cute as a girl," another girl said. She looked to be about eighteen.

"We are here," said Sara, interrupting them. All the girls, as well as Zidika, turned to look at the dark castle that stood before them.

***

This is all a dream! thought Rena. *This isn't reality. It's all a lie. An illusion. I want to see them! I want to see all of them again! I want to see Zidika and tell him my feelings. I want to feel his lips against mine and feel his soft skin and run my hand through his hair. I just want to see his smiling face again.* "I want to see everyone! Zidika!" she yelled, as she awakened from her dream.

***

Just as Zidika jumped off the dragon and landed on the castle battlements, Sara joined him, followed by all of the other girls.

"It's over," Sara said as she stood on one of the castle towers, a dead look on her face. Rena ran over to Zidika. He just smiled.

"No, it's over for you," said Aegleca. A thorn shot in front of Sara and stabbed her through her chest, close to her heart. Sara started coughing up blood. Blood ran from her eyes. A lethal poison had been placed on the thorn, and Sara could not escape its deadly intent. She fell off the tower and landed on the ground.

"No!" Rena yelled. She held her hands out and used her water power to create a bed underneath Sara to soften her landing. It evaporated when Sara gently hit the ground. Rena felt as if her heart had just stopped. Everyone stood still for a minute. Then they all rushed down the steps.

They saw Sara coughing out blood; there was blood all around her. Zidika ran to her. He lifted her head off the ground. "Sara! Sara," he whispered to her. She was stiff, and her body was cold. Rena stood a few feet behind Zidika, staring at the scene in horror.

"Rena, I'm glad you're okay," Sara said slowly as blood dripped from her mouth. "And, Zidika, you have been a good boy."

"Oh, Sara, don't speak. You'll make it worse," said Zidika.

"At least I got to see him one last time before I died," she said, raising her hand and pointing at the castle. "I want you to know this: I have always loved you, no matter what they said. You never left my heart." She smiled one of those bright, beautiful smiles. But it was filled with death. Death followed her smile.

CHAPTER 21

Sara's Death

• • • • • • • • • • • •

Her body was cold. She was motionless. Her hand dropped to her side. Blood was all over her. She lay in her own blood. Her smiling face disappeared forever. Her heart had stopped.

Zidika did not move. He did not force himself to transform, but his eyes turned blood red. He did not break down in tears and cry. He just stood there, frozen as a stone, his trembling hands holding her fragile body, her lifeless body, because that was all he could do. He couldn't hear anything. Everything was a blur, and he did not see or hear what Rena was saying. He heard the crying of the humans and the howling of the moon. But at the same time, he could sense and hear other things. He had heard Sara's last heartbeat. He had heard her last breath and had known it would be her last. Her warm blood had turned ice cold. Her rosy cheeks had tuned pale as the warmth escaped her body, leaving nothing behind but an empty shell. It was a full moon that night, and even in his agitated state, he still noticed it. He thought about the memorys they shared and thought that she would love to watch the moon with him as they had done before. But now everything was silent. He stood there holding her beautiful body—the body from which all life had faded. He knew it would now turn into a pile of bones. He looked into her lifeless eyes. There were still so many things he wanted to do with her, say to her. He wanted her to be with him and Rena. He wanted her to be there when finally told Rena how much she meant to him. And she would smile one of the biggest, brightest smiles he would ever see.

But the last smile she had given him hadn't been like that. It had been filled with sadness. His heart wanted to cry. It hadn't been the sort of smile that comforted him and filled him with happiness as her previous smiles had done. A cold, dark, sad, painful feeling suffocated him now because he knew it had been her last smile. It had been the last bright and beautiful smile he would ever see from her. He saw in her smile how much she wanted to stay. Her voice had been filled with such emotion that he felt his heart breaking.

The girls behind Rena were also crying and holding each other in their grief. Tears suffocated Rena. Even though she had just met Sara, even though she sometimes found her annoying, she felt as if they had become close friends. When Sara smiled at them she knew that it would be her last and it was killing her. She was dying on the inside. She covered her mouth with both of her hands as tears ran down her cheeks.

Celesta appeared with the other unicorns and looked at the body. The creatures stopped and looked sadly down at Sara and Zidika. A tear fell from Celesta's eyes, and Zidika felt it land on his arm.

Rena backed away as the pain continued. The guilt and all the other emotions of her father's death built up inside of her. "Not again," she whispered. Her voice was filled with so much emotion. "It's all because of me." Everyone stopped and looked at her. Rena just kept backing up. "I'm the one who killed her," she said loudly. "I'm the one who got captured. If you all hadn't come to save me, this wouldn't have happened. Sara would still be alive. And my father would still be alive. I killed both of them. Why did you come and save me?" she yelled. The pain and guilt were eating her. She couldn't escape it.

Zidika set Sara gently on the ground and walked up to Rena. He took her in his arms and pulled her close. "It's all my fault," she said, weeping.

"No, it's not," Zidika said, holding her closer.

"Don't try to defend me," she yelled. She broke loose from Zidika and ran away.

Zidika grabbed her arm and pulled her back. "No! Stop it!" she yelled. With a great force, she used both of her hands to thrust Zidika back. "You cannot change what has been done," Rena said, her eyes motionless.

CHAPTER 22

Deep Dreams

. . . .

So warm. Why is it so warm? Rena was surrounded in a yellow light. All around her, white puffy lights were flying up. All she saw was the yellow light. *Why do I feel so peaceful? Why do I feel so calm? What happened to me? Where am I?* Rena looked around and smiled, her mind totally free.

Who cares? It is so calming here.

The yellow light circled around Rena. It surrounded her completely as it lifted her a few feet off the ground. Her hair turned black and flared up. Her eyes turned blood red. A great wind blew across the field sending everything flying. Rena lifted up her hands with such a great force that the ground started trembling, causing everything in the area to shatter. Stars aligned and then, one by one, started shattering. Little yellow sparkles of light started falling from the sky to the ground.

All Rena's powers started combining together. Everyone looked up and saw the stars shattering. "What's going on here?" asked one of the girls.

"I don't know," said Zidika. "If Sara were here, she would know."

Suddenly they heard a rumbling noise. They looked behind them. The castle shattered and crumbled to the ground. Everything shattered like a mirror, like a piece of glass thrown to the floor. Everything broke into a million tiny pieces that could never be put together ever again. Even the grass was ripped from the ground and shredded into tiny pieces. Nothing was in its right place. Everything was out of whack. Even the seasons started changing. A blizzard was created, and then, out of nowhere, fire appeared. No one could do anything to stop Rena now.

"Why am I here?" Rena asked herself again. This time a white light swirled around her.

Soon a woman appeared, wearing a long white dress. She smiled so beautifully at Rena. "You do not belong here, Rena." She spoke in an angelic voice.

"Why am I not supposed to be here? Where am I supposed to be then?"

"Your wish to escape everything—to escape the guilt—was granted, and you ended up in this place, where time has stopped for you. You let all your anger, hatred, and sadness, take over your consciousness. Now both worlds are in grave danger. Rena, you must wake up. You do not belong in this place."

"Rena!" She heard a familiar voice. The woman vanished, and Rena turned around to see him. "Rena!"

"Zidika!" They hugged each other tightly. Rena looked up into his eyes, his beautiful hazel eyes. They sparkled so brightly.

"Rena, you've got to wake up. We all need you, Rena. Wake up. Don't ever leave me."

"Zidika, I won't ever leave you." Suddenly everything around her vanished. The warm feeling, the bright yellow light, Zidika. Everything around her had gone, and she found herself in a dark place.

"What happened to her?" one of the girls asked as Rena fell to the ground.

Zidika ran to her and lifted her head off the ground. "It was too much for her," he said softly. "She couldn't take it anymore," he said, trying to push back the tears. "I still didn't get to tell her how I felt!" he yelled, pulling her closer. He soon found himself in a different dimension. He was in a dark and gloomy place. Then he saw the person he had wanted to see most of all, the one and only person who warmed his heart. Rena lay in the middle of the place, her body floating up. Zidika walked over to her, and his face hovered over hers.

Rena opened her eyes slowly and saw a blurry vision of Zidika. Her eyes widened when she realized it was him. She stood up and smiled the brightest smile he had ever seen from her. "You came for me!"

"How could I leave you?" She hugged him tightly. "I love you, Rena." he said squeezing her.

"And I love you too." They looked at each other one last time before they realized they were back in their own bodies. Rena carefully got up as Zidika still held on to her. Everyone was so amazed, so happy to see both of them.

Everything around them began to turn back to normal. New stars appeared in the sky, and the grass started growing back. The blizzard and the fire vanished. Everything was as it was before, except that the castle was still shattered. Then they all heard a voice behind them.

"I didn't expect this to happen," said Aegleca. I didn't expect for you to have so much power that you could even shatter the stars. I didn't expect for Sara to say that she still loved me. I didn't know any of this would happen."

Zidika looked at Aegleca angrily as he got up and started to walk toward him, but Rena stopped him. She got up and walked over to him. Her face looked peaceful, as if she had forgiven him already.

"We do not expect many the things that happen in our lives," said Rena. "We may have it planned out till the very end, but always, things turn out totally different from what we expect. We cannot take back the mistakes that we have made. All we can do it learn from them. Our lives will be filled with hardships and failure, but that is what makes us better people.

I learned that the hard way." She lifted up the disappointed demon from the ground and hugged him. "What happened today was not your fault. Do not blame yourself." She looked at him and saw the demon smile. The other half of his face retuned, and he looked handsome.

"You truly are like Sara," said Aegleca. "I loved her till the very end. But my hatred and revenge toward her people kept me from seeing the truth. Thank you, young lady, for helping me find the truth once more." Rena smiled happily, and it was as if Sara was smiling too, and the demon saw that she smiled like Sara.

"Now that you have no feelings of hatred toward us, can you release your possession on the centipede called Mukade?" asked Rena.

"I will do as you ask, but I cannot tell what its next steps will be. I may have possessed the demon, but I cannot tell it what to do after I release it. You understand that, right?"

Rena looked sweetly at him. "I know. At least you won't have it under your control, and it will be free to do whatever it wants."

The demon nodded. He closed his eyes and mouthed some words and made some hand signs. Suddenly the atmosphere changed, and Rena felt and evil aura. A dangerous presence was heading her way—and very fast.

CHAPTER 23

Rena's Dream

. . . .

"Stand guard! It shall come! Everybody, try your best!" Rena shouted as the ground trembled. Then, from underneath the ground, Mukade thrust himself out and screeched with a terrifying voice. The demon's true colors were shown: red, yellow, and black. It lunged at Rena, its venomous pincers ready to attack, and Rena was getting ready to use her water powers to block it when suddenly the demon Aegleca stepped in front of her.

"No!" Rena yelled as Mukade's needle-like pincers shot though him. They ripped through his organs and slithered right to his heart. Rena ran up to him and knelt down beside him. "Why did you do that?" she asked, trying not to cry.

He just smiled at her for the first time. "I must pay for what I done."

"No! Taking your own life won't solve anything. You should have lived. Then you could have made a difference." Rena held his bloody hands, and her tears dripped onto his fingers.

He smiled once more—a bright warm smile. "At least now I can be with her. Sara, we can be together." He was still smiling when he closed his eyes forever. A bright light surrounded him and Rena, and she saw him with Sara. They were happily walking away together. They turned and waved goodbye to Rena. She smiled back sadly as her tears flowed down. "I'll never forget you," she whispered.

CHAPTER 24

True Colors

· · · · · · · · · · ·

"**J**ust because I'm free doesn't mean I will give you back your brother," the centipede hissed. "In fact, he turned out to be quite useful."

Rena was filled with so much emotion when she heard that. What had Joey been forced to do? Destroy villages? People's lives? The thought of that made her sick. "Let's test that theory out." Rena held out her hands, and water shot out in two streams that joined together and became one big, powerful stream. It smashed into the centipede, and Rena then let out fire. Flames flew toward the centipede. They vanished and turned to black just before they reached the demon. Joey's sword came out of nowhere, casing the flame to dissolve.

How is that possible? Thought Rena. *Nothing is supposed to escape from that flame until everything disappears—until I want it to!*

Joey came out from the shadows and looked at Rena in hatred and anger. He looked as if he was angry with her for something. She had never seen her brother look at her that way.

"Good," said the centipede as Joey walked next to it. "Now tear this girl into pieces, and this time finish the job!" Joey nodded and ran forward.

Rena called out to the others. "I can't fight both of them at once! You fight the centipede, and I'll deal with my brother." Everyone nodded. The unicorns came charging, and even Kiche came to help. He flew up into the air and helped the unicorns to escape before they were attacked. All the girls concentrated their attacks on the centipede, but their efforts didn't seem to do anything.

Joey's long sword came rushing at Rena. She used her water powers to shield herself from his attack. She no longer had Sara's sword with her. "Joey!" Rena shouted. "Why can't you hear me? I know that, on the inside, you don't want this. I know that you're that scared little boy who needed my help—who asked me to save him." Rena kept using her powers to shield herself from his attacks. Why wasn't he responding? Could he really … No, she didn't want to think about it. She was going to get her brother back no matter what it took.

"Joey, please!" Rena was backing away. His attacks were too strong, and she knew it would be impossible for her to hold on much longer. "Joey!" she shouted one last time before she fell. Joey thrust his sword at her, and Rena couldn't get up in time to block it. She closed her eyes so she wouldn't see her own brother doing this. Just then she heard the sound of two swords crashing against each other. She opened her eyes to see Zidika with a knife.

"Rena, get up!" yelled Zidika. "You're the only one who can do this, Rena, so get up." That gave Rena the courage to continue. She stood up and walked over to Joey. His raised sword was still being blocked by Zidika, and Joey couldn't advance for another attack. Rena grabbed Joey's sword and forced it down with all of her strength. Once the sword was on the ground, Rena did the one thing no one would have thought she would do. She held her hands out. "Come, Joey," she said sweetly as she smiled a bright smile.

That was when Joey remembered. That smile. It was Rena's.

Mukade the centipede was trying its best to keep its hold on Joey, and it almost succeeded, but when Rena saw that Joey's eyes were becoming redder, she pulled him closer. "I'm sorry, Joey," she said patting his head. Joey tried to pull away, but Rena held him tighter. "I was not the only one hurt. You were hurt too. I didn't see that. I thought I hurt more than anyone. I thought I was the one to blame, but I was wrong. It was no one's fault for what had happened." He felt warm and comforted by her touch and the warmth of her body as she wrapped her arms around him. Rena looked at her brother. "I may not know the reason that Father died, but I do know that everything happens for a reason. So that's why I need you to come back. Joey, I need you to come back to me. Everyone's waiting." She held out a hand to him.

Joeys motionless, colorless eyes began to change, and they soon became their vivid original color again. The sword also disappeared. When Joey regained consciousness, he saw only his beautiful, bright, and happy sister looking at him. He smiled the brightest smile Rena had ever seen. He ran into her arms. "Joey, welcome back."

"It's good to be back."

CHAPTER 25

Blossom

· · · · · · · · ·

J oey was free, but they needed to kill the centipede. Rena looked a Joey and was happy that he was back. Then she focused her attention back at the creature. All of the girls had used all their power, strength, and everything they had learned, but none of that seemed to have worked.

"What is that thing?" Joey asked, terrified.

Rena look at him. She could hardly believe him. How could he not remember everything that had happened? "Don't you remember, Joey?"

"No, why should I? Is it something important?" Joey looked around and saw that he was not at home. "Where am I? And what am I doing here? What are you doing here? And what's up with all these strange things? Like unicorns and a dragon and the girls with their powers. Rena, what is going on here?" Joey wanted answers to all these questions. They captured his mind and wouldn't to let go.

Rena looked at him, amazed that he did not remember a single thing that had happened to him during the past few weeks. Maybe his memory was erased when he was freed from the possession of the centipede. Rena pushed Joey out of her way to Zidika so he wouldn't get hurt.

The demon centipede Mukade looked toward them and screeched. Then it aimed its venomous pincers strait for them. Rena used her hands to shield them. Water shot out of her hands and created a barrier. "Stay here, Joey!" she demanded. "Don't even think about moving from this spot." Joey did not understand what was going on, but he nodded. Rena ran forward. She held her hands out, maintaining the water shield with her water powers to prevent the attacks of the centipede. Soon the water shield transformed into a weapon—a long spear with a really pointy tip. Holding it up, she used her ice powers to cover it with layer of ice to thicken it. She then used her fire power to create a small ball of flame at the tip of the new weapon.

She ran to where the girls were standing and told them to back up. She threw the spear forward. With that, she created a small yellow ball that lifted her up into the air. She used all three of her powers and all the strength she had for this final attack. If it didn't work, she wouldn't know what to do. The combination of all of her powers together created one big ball of light that swirled with snow, water, fire, lightening, and dark fire. The ball of light shot it out as the spear came in contact with Mukade. He screeched his last cry and fell to his demise.

Joey did not know what was going on, but he had to admit that his sister was amazing. Rena landed back on the ground. She was so happy and relieved that the battle was all over and they could now finally go back home and finally be with everyone—their parents and family members and friends. They both wanted to go back to the place they called home. Rena was so happy she wanted to cheer—until she remembered what she would be leaving behind when she left.

Everyone else cheered in victory, happy that everything was over and okay. Rena looked at Joey, and then her gaze fell upon Zidika as he walked up to her. She ran up to him and into his arms.

"We did it!" she said happily. "We can finally go back!"

Zidika's smile faded, and Rena realized that he didn't want her to leave. She started laughing in order to hold back her tears.

Zidika gave her a sad smile. "Don't worry, Rena," he said, pushing her hair out of her face. He gave her a quick kiss. "You finally did it! You got what you came here for. Now return where you belong."

"But, Zidika …" she said, trying not to tear up. She saw that it was hard on him too. "Did you mean it? What you told me. Do you really mean it?"

"Yes." He gave her another kiss before he set her down to the ground.

Rena looked sadly away as she walked to where the girls were still gathered. "Thank you, everyone, for coming to save me. I thank you from the bottom of my heart. But I must leave now."

Then a little girl came up to her. She wore her black hair in pigtails, and her eyes were the color of hazel nuts. "Will you come back, miss?"

Rena looked at her sadly and forced a smile. "I'm sorry, but I will not be returning."

The girl looked sadly at Rena. "But why not?" she asked.

"Because where I come from is my home. But I will say that I will miss you guys—all of you. But I must return home."

The girls nodded in understanding. Many of them mounted their unicorns, and the others climbed onto Kiche with Zidika, Rena, and Jocy. Rena was sad to leave this place. She had grown to love it so much. And the person she would miss most of all was the person who had taught her to love again and to be herself. Before her arrival there, she had been like a flower waiting to blossom, and now she had. She understood that what she had could be easily taken away from her. She had never understood what it was really like to be alone and sad and lost, but Zidika had, because he had been through experiences that taught him.

She understood now what she had been missing—her old self, and not just that.

CHAPTER 26

A Mermaid's Spell

· · · · · · · · · · · · · · · · · ·

After dropping off the girls, Rena and Zidika and Kiche flew back up into the air. Joey had wanted to ride the unicorns. Rena had been hesitant at first, but then she let him. She watched him eagerly as he enjoyed himself. He was riding Celesta, so she wasn't too worried that something might happen. Then she suddenly remembered. "Oh, my goodness!" she said.

Zidika turned to look at her a little worried. "What is it?"

"How could I forget something so important? That girl! I promised Rin I would save her!" *How could I forget something like that?* she thought. *It was an important promise I made to Rin.*

"Rena, you just finished a big battle—"

But she did not let him finish. "Zidika, I made a promise to the girl called Rin. I can't just go back on my word." She looked at him seriously. Zidika sighed giving in. "I was told that the place was close to where we were, so the village must be that one since it's the only one I can see." She pointed down to a tiny town below them. "Kiche, take us down please." Kiche did as he was told. He landed on the ground far enough away from the village so that the people there wouldn't see him.

Rena slid off, and so did Zidika. Rena asked Kiche to look after Joey until she returned. He agreed with a nod. If any harm came to Joey, she didn't know how she would deal with it.

When she walked into the village with Zidika, the place seemed to be deserted. No one was around. They didn't see anything—not a single person. The wind blew freely, however. "What's up with this place? It's like a ghost town," Zidika said looking at an old fallen sign.

"How am I supposed to find the girl?" said Rena. "There is no one here!"

"No, they're just hiding," said Zidika as he suddenly ran after the shadow of a person he had seen hiding behind one of the old houses. Rena watched him as he disappeared behind the house. She waited for him to return, but he didn't. She was starting to get worried as she looked around. Still she didn't see him. She looked at the ground behind her and saw a shadow. She turned around, holding her hands out, but she was too late. Someone grabbed both her hands and knocked her to the ground. Soon everything around her went blank.

Rena woke up hearing noises around her. She kept her head on the ground but noticed that her feet and hands were tied, she was blindfolded. Someone must have been holding onto the long piece of rope that was tied around her hands because she felt a tug on it as soon as she awoke. "Hey, looks like the little birdy woke up!" said someone, laughing. Other people whom Rena hadn't known were there joined in the loud laughter. This really annoyed her. Rena felt the rope biting her and ripping though her skin as the man pulled on it. He ordered her to get up. She had trouble getting up since her feet and hands were tied and she couldn't see, but he ordered some of the men to bring her to him and take off the ropes. They did as they were told. Rena tried kicking, but it didn't work. When they finally took the blindfold from her eyes, Rena spoke in an angry tone. "What is this this? Where am I?"

"Oh, look! She wants answers," the one who appeared to be the leader said.

Rena got down right to business. "Are you guys holding a captive girl who is called Jada?"

The leader stopped smiling and stood up. "How on earth do you know her?" He spoke in a tone that frightened her. Then she heard voices. When she turned and focused her attention on the voices, she saw someone bringing Zidika in. He was struggling to get lose. "Let go of me!" he yelled.

"Zidika!" Rena ran up to him.

Zidika looked surprised to see her. "Rena, what happened to you? Did they hurt you?"

"No. What about you?"

"Don't worry about me."

"I take it that you already know each other," said the leader as he approached Rena. "I shall take you to Jada, but how she'll deal with you is up to her." His response surprised Rena. He took Rena by the hand and pulled her out of the house where she had been held captive. He led her into a much larger house, and then he immediately left.

"Who is this?" A gentle and sweet voice spoke, but with force. The girl was hidden behind a huge cloth that covered half of the room. Rena could not see her.

"I am Rena. I have come here to rescue you from here and take you back to your village. I have been sent here by a girl named Rin."

"Rin? Rin? You know where … oh, tell me, how is she?" The girl's voice seemed to have changed. It sounded much happier and without strain.

"You will find out yourself after I free you from your captors."

"No! No, you do not understand. They haven't captured me."

"But I have been told—"

But the girl did not let her finish. "It is true that they took me against my will, but they have been so kind and nice to me. They let me do anything I please. It is almost like being free."

"But you aren't free! Jada, come with me. I will return you back to your village, and then you will truly be free."

"How do you know that name?"

"Rin told me."

"How could she? She knows what that name could do to me."

"But doesn't that name mean celestial star?"

"But in different language it means Abaddon."

"Who are you then?"

"I am not a human; neither am I a demon."

"Can that mean that you are half human and half demon?"

"You are correct."

"May I please see you?"

"No! Don't get any closer to me!" Jada suddenly shouted, but Rena did not listen. She walked up and pushed away the curtain to reveal a girl with long, blond, curly hair and sparkling, big, blue eyes. Diamonds sparkled in her hair and on her skin beneath her eyes. Her forehead was covered in pink, blue, and purple scales. She wore a purple cloak and a dark green dress. She sat in a pool of water, and Rena saw a pink-and-purple tail popping out. "Why didn't you listen to me?" cried Jada. "Why did you insist on seeing me?"

"You're a mermaid!" said Rena. "Ever since I came here, I have seen such beautiful and amazing things—things that I thought couldn't be possible! Now I will believe anything I see." She walked closer.

"No! Don't come any closer." But Rena did not listen. She walked forward as if under a spell. A grey color began to swirl in her eyes. *What's happening to me?* she thought. *Why can't I seem to take control?* Rena got into the pool of water with the mermaid and touched her scaly tail. *Am I being controlled?* she thought. *No, it seems the mermaid doesn't want this.*

Jada the mermaid tried to get out of the water, but then something drew her to Rena. Jada's eyes sparkled dangerously. Rena's blood smelled so sweet and nice, so warm and tender. She wanted taste that blood. She touched Rena's cheek and then leaned against her neck. The blood smelled nice. She craved it. She showed her sharp teeth before she bit down into Rena's neck and drank her blood.

Rena felt the sharp pain, and the blood was drained out of her too quickly. She wanted it to stop, but she couldn't move. She couldn't break loose from this spell.

"No!" She heard Jada cry out and felt a tear fall from Jada's eyes onto her skin, but Jada couldn't seem to stop herself. She tried to pull herself away from Rena, but somehow was drawn back in.

***

"What's going on here? Where did you take Rena?"

"The mermaid's room," said the captain.

"But I have heard only legends about mermaids. There can't be any still be alive."

"She is the last remaining one."

"Oh, no! That can't be good." He got up to leave, but the men tried to stop him. He took out his knife and pushed them away as he ran out of the room to Rena.

***

Rena felt herself fading. She felt weak and dizzy. She brought her hands up, but set them back down. She was too weak to even hold them up. *Why is this happening? Why is this happening to me? Why can't I stop her? Why can't I do anything? I finally got Joey back … I am so close. Why can't I stop her? Why am I so weak?* No, she wasn't going to be like this. She wasn't going to let it all end like this. She was not the person she had been before. She was stronger now. "No!" she yelled as she used a great force to tear herself away from the mermaid's grasp. The mermaid flew back away from the pool of water. Her tail soon disappeared, and Rena saw only two feet. Blood was all over Jada's mouth, and Rena touched her neck and looked at her hand. Blood quickly spread everywhere. Rena was trying to use a bit of the curtain to cover her neck when Zidika arrived. He quickly tied his shirt around her neck. He then took her into his arms as she nuzzled her head into his chest. When he was finally able to get her to her feet, he started to lead her out of the house, but Rena suddenly spoke. "The girl—we need to get her and bring her back! She does not belong here."

"Are you kidding me? After what she did to you?"

"Please, Zidika," Rena begged in a weak voice. Then she closed her eyes. Zidika looked back at the unconscious girl.

CHAPTER 27

Don't Cry

• • • • • • • • • • •

Rena slept for three days. Zidika remained at her side for the whole time. He watched her sleep. She was beautiful. As the sun rose above the eastern horizon, rays of light streamed through window and rained down onto Rena's hair, bringing out the bright-blond color and also the red that had stained her hair a little. As she was bathed in the warm light, she looked so peaceful, and Zidika wondered if she could be any more beautiful. He stood and stared as she slept, and then he walked out. He wasn't worried. Rena was a strong girl.

When Rena finally woke up from her sleep, she didn't know how much time had passed. She stood up and stretched her arms. Then she noticed someone sitting next to her curled up into a ball, with her head tucked in. It was the girl. She walked up to the girl and smiled. "I'm glad," she told her.

"I'm sorry," Jada said suddenly as she looked up at Rena.

"For what?" Rena stood up as if she did not understand.

"Don't you get it? For what I tried to do to you! Aren't you upset? Why aren't you mad at me?"

"Is that what you want?"

"What?"

"I mean, I'm not judging you for what you did, but you don't seem to want to leave me alone about it. Do you want me to be mad at you? Do you want me to hate you?"

Jada looked down, ashamed. "No. I don't want to be hated. I don't want to be forgotten."

"Then don't bring up the subject again. The reason I don't hate you is that I can see that it wasn't your fault. It was an accident." She smiled, but Jada looked away.

"That only happens when I'm in the water," Jada explained.

"Why did those guys let you leave so easily?"

"Oh, a sleeping spell. When they wake up, they won't remember me ever being there."

"So, if you had that kind of power, why didn't you use it before—to escape?"

"Because I thought they were protecting me. They were hiding me from the world because I'm the last of my kind. But you know what? I don't want to be hidden from the world. I don't want to run and always keep hiding. That's what we mermaids have always done. We were born part human and part fish, as you have witnessed. We traveled a long distance to finally find a place to call home. We have to be in the water a little bit every hour. If we are not, our feet dry up. If anyone sees us in the water, they are put under a spell immediately. Even if we don't want to be, we are drawn to human blood. I am the last remaining mermaid. I am Queen Jada. I came to Rin's village to start a new life. I never told anyone my secret. I was afraid that maybe they would chase me out. I was in the water, and Rin accidently saw me when she came to fetch water. I was afraid. I thought that she would be put under the spell and then I would have to leave, but instead, she was not put under the spell. I do not know how that was possible, but she did not run away. She was interested in me, and she asked me many questions, which I enjoyed answering. We became very close and spent a lot of time together. Whenever I went to the river, she would always be on guard to make sure no one would see me." She looked at Rena. "I'm through with running away. I'm not going to run anymore."

"The first thing to do is return to the village," Rena said. "I bet Rin misses you dearly, and so do the other villagers. Then you could live the life you want to. You don't have to let anyone tell you live it any differently."

Jada walked up to Rena and put her hands close to her. She closed her eyes and concentrated on something. Then she spoke, keeping her eyes closed. "I feel that you have changed. You used to be someone else, but now you are you." She opened her eyes. They both smiled at each other.

"Oh, I almost forgot," Jada said. "Zidika asked me to tell you to meet him outside, but he also wants you to wear that." She pointed to a white dress. Rena smiled, picked up the dress, and held it in her hands. The fabric was soft and neatly woven. The dress was long and had spaghetti straps. A narrow silver rope was tied around the waist, and it reflected the light. Rena decided to try it on. It fit perfectly; she had her mother's figure—the body of a model. She loved the dress and how it looked on her. It was so beautiful that she couldn't stop admiring it. How could such a beautiful thing be created when the people in this world wore clothing that was so old fashioned? This dress looked like something she could buy in the shops at home—except the stitching was different and the fabric was like none she had ever seen. The dress had been sewn by hand, but it looked like a professional's handiwork. But all of this brought her thoughts back to her real world, and she remembered that she would soon be leaving this place. She was upset as she thought about it.

She peeked outside and saw Joey playing with Celesta. She felt comfortable knowing that he was all right and happy. He was laughing and smiling so brightly that her heart was filled with positive emotions. It made her happy to see him this happy.

Just then Zidika walked in. He saw Rena wearing the dress and smiled. "You're finally awake," he said.

"How long was I asleep?"

"Three days."

"That long? But how?"

"That doesn't matter," he said. "That dress looks perfect on you." He paused for a second. "Come, let's take a walk."

"I'll go change."

"No, what you're wearing now is perfect." They laced their hands together and walked outside. Rena looked at Joey for a second and smiled. Celesta would protect him with her life if any danger came near him, so she wasn't that worried about leaving him for a while. They walked down the path until they came to a waterfall. "I remember taking a walk and seeing a girl sleeping here," said Zidika.

Rena turned completely red when she remembered. But Zidika didn't seem to notice. "Why are you telling me this?"

"Because I remember thinking that she looked beautiful in the moonlight, and for some strange reason, I thought of you. She reminded me of you, and then after that, it got light, and I couldn't stop thinking of you. Rena, when we first met, you made an impression on me like no one else ever did. And then I couldn't stop thinking of you." He led her off the path, and Rena started to recall the place. "This is where you were attacked."

"You remembered. Yeah," she said, "this is also the place where you saved me. I don't see why we had to come here."

"Because I wanted to show you something, halfling."

Rena stopped walking. She crossed her arms and stared at him. "Why did you call me halfling?"

He smiled as if expecting for that question. "Because you look like a fairy standing there in that dress. The sun is bringing out the light in your eyes. You are a fairy—my queen fairy."

Rena smiled brightly. "And you are my fairy king!" She put her arm around his waist, and he put his arm around her shoulder and pulled her closer. Now Rena knew—she knew his answer. He had chosen her.

They walked along until they came to a cave. The small opening was barely big enough for two people, but when Rena got inside, she saw that the interior was much bigger than she expected. "Wow! It's so beautiful!" It all came to her as a surprise; she had never seen anything like it. All around her the walls were covered in tiny purple rocks that glittered and shone in the sunlight that came into the cave through an opening high in the ceiling. A large blanket was laid out in the middle of the area, and she saw a basket that contained fruits and flowers. "This almost feels like a date," Rena said when she sat down.

"A date," Zidika said, which only made him smile more. He picked up the red roses and put them in her hair. Rena lay down and stared up at the brightly sparkling purple rocks. She wanted to remember this time always. She wanted to spend as much time there as she could before she … A frown grew on her face.

Zidika sat up looking at her worried. "What is it?" he asked.

"It's just that, when I leave, I will never see you again."

Zidika touched her check and turned her head toward him. "Why do you say that?"

"Because only people who originally came from my world can travel back to it. I know that because Sara told me." She tried to hold back tears.

"Don't be sad over something like that. You've got to enjoy this moment. Enjoy it for as long as you can before it ends."

"But I can't leave you, Zidika. I love you!"

"And I love you." He kissed her, and Rena could smell the fresh leaves and the fragrant earth on him. It smelled nice, and she wished she could always inhale it.

"We will meet again. I promise you that." He looked at her and gave her another one of his charming smiles. "Promise me you won't be upset. Promise me you will keep on smiling."

Rena looked up at him, and a smile grew on her face. "You're right." Then she lay back down with him, and they both stared up into the sparkling ceiling.

CHAPTER 28

Goodbye

· · · · · · · ·

All her life, Rena had taken things for granted. She never realized that she was lucky to have what she had. She never realized that she should be grateful because not a lot of people had what she had. She shouldn't have blamed herself. She shouldn't have hated anyone. She was running away from the world. All her life she had known only one life, and she had lived by the rules that were given to her. It was like looking though a crystal and seeing only one place. But by looking through a different facet of the crystal, another place becomes visible. There are different worlds out there that are totality different from one another. Rena thought that, to get through life, she could never show people that she was weak. All she wanted was to love and be loved by someone, and now, since she had that, her eyes had opened. She could now see the world though different sides of the crystal. She was finally able to act like herself. She no longer needed to act like the quiet girl. She was no longer afraid of getting hurt. She was no longer running away from her problems; rather, she was facing them. Now she could be herself. She had finally found the place where she thought she belonged. She was truly a flower that had blossomed.

It was dark by the time Zidika returned with Rena. They talked and laughed. Rena looked happy, and she wanted to stay that way. She had spent the whole day with Zidika, and she wanted life to always be like that. She had felt his warm touch, and it still lingered. She wanted it to last forever. She didn't want to leave. Maybe she could …

Joey ran up to Rena smiling so happily. He told her that Jada had left for her village. Rena was happy to hear that. How could she stay here now that she had found Joey after having looked for him all of that time? How could she stay when she knew she needed to go back with Joey because everyone on the other side was waiting for them? She could not think selfish thoughts. But it still hurt. Her heart hurt because she knew that this could be the last time she would spend with Zidika, her fairy king.

They spent the night at his house, and in the morning, they got ready to leave. Rena changed into her blue tank top and black jeans. She walked over to Zidika. "Thanks for everything." She looked down, trying not to look upset. This was their last time together, and Rena felt as if her heart was breaking. She felt as if a piece of her was dying.

Zidika lifted her head up. "Don't look so down, Rena." He handed her the white dress, which was neatly folded. On top of it lay a sliver chain from which hung a small charm in the shape of a leaf. For some reason, Rena felt as if she had seen it before, but then that thought just vanished.

"Keep it. I don't expect anything in return." Rena smiled trying not to look so down. "Promise me that we will meet again," she said seriously. "Promise me that, and then I can leave in peace."

Zidika looked straight into her eyes. She noticed that his amber eyes looked so beautiful, and the light made them sparkle. She saw her reflection in his eyes, and he didn't need to say a word because she already knew. "Rena, we will meet again soon. You can count on that. I promise you that we will not be apart for long."

Rena smiled brightly. Her smile was full of sunshine and hope. That's all that she needed to hear. Now everything would be as it was before. No, nothing would be the same.

Rena walked up to the mirror. She stopped. The mirror was right in front of them. She could see it, and she knew that Joey could see it. But she realized that Zidika didn't seem to notice it. He actually seemed to be wondering why Rena had suddenly stopped.

"Well, here's my stop." She turned to look at Zidika and tried to hold back the tears. "This is the legendary sonic mirror. It may be invisible to you because you haven't traveled through it. But my brother and I can see it well. I will be going through this mirror and back to my own time." Zidika smiled, and Rena again wondered if he could see it.

"Do we have to leave now?" Joey whined.

Rena knelt down beside Joey and gave him a friendly smile. "Yes. Everyone will be waiting for us on the other side. Think about Mom, our friends, and our grandparents. Think about what they must be feeling." She flinched at her own words. Those words almost sounded as if they had been slightly forced out of her.

Tears whelmed up in Joey's eyes, and he started crying as he hugged Rena. "I'm sorry, Rena. I didn't mean to be selfish. I will do whatever you say. I miss everyone already."

Rena hugged him back. *Poor Joey*, she thought. *He has already been through enough*. She pulled back from him and looked into his eyes. "I know you love this place, and I do too, but you do know we do not belong here. When we get back home, don't mention this to anybody, okay?" Joey nodded in agreement he whipped away his tears and tried to look happily at Rena.

Rena stood up and looked at Zidika one last time. "Well, then, I shall be going." She smiled a sunny smile and flashed him a wave before she stepped into the mirror. She held onto her brother tightly as they passed through many mirrors with great speed. Once they stopped, Joey wanted to run out, but Rena pulled him back. She remembered the last time she had tried to do that. She had fallen into a dark space as if she was floating in time. She tried to think of a way to get out without falling into that same place this time. But just then, Joey tugged on her tank top. "It's okay, sister." He put his hands together, and a red glow came out creating a path. He stepped onto it, and it took him into the other side with no problem. Rena did the same. They came out of the mirror. She looked at the mirror, but no longer saw herself with red hair and armor. It was just her. Sara was no longer with her. She was truly herself—her own person. She frowned a little, but she was happy to know that Sara was in a better place—a much better place than being trapped within Rena's body. But also Rena thought about that demon. Sara had never told her why she possessed all three of the powers, but maybe she didn't want to know. Maybe it was best that she didn't know.

Rena turned the symbol to seal the mirror, and then she covered it up with sheets. She grabbed her brother's hand, and together they ran out of the shed.

***

Zidika stared at the mirror. He could see it perfectly; he had just pretended not to be able to see it. "Guess Sara was right," he said.

"About what?" Celesta asked.

"That Rena would help me find the mirror."

"Why didn't you go with her?" Celesta asked.

"I guess I wasn't ready." And he turned around and left.

CHAPTER 29

Back Home

. . . .

Zidika sat in his little cottage thinking about her—about Rena. He thought about everything that had happened to him since he met her. How much had he changed since then? And then his memory brought him to the distant past. Now he knew why—now he remembered why he had thought he knew her, why she had looked so familiar. It was not because she had Sara in her. No, that was only a little part of it. The answer was so simple: he had met her before. He had met an eleven-year-old Rena in the park. She had been singing a little song, and every day for a while after that first day, they would meet each other in the park and would always find themselves talking about all kinds of things. They always had fun. But one day she didn't come. He waited for her, but she didn't come the next day or the next day. But he still waited for her because, after all, Rena was his first love. He waited for her because he wanted to give her something—a silver leaf charm on a silver chain. His brother had given it to him, and it was because of that necklace that he had met Rena. He wanted to give her that necklace. But he never saw her again, she never did come to the park again. That was Rena—the sweet, quiet eleven-year-old girl he had fallen in love with so long ago.

***

Rena felt herself stop when she opened the shed to the outside world. The sun was too bright when it suddenly shone on them. It seemed as if she hadn't seen the bright light in a while; rather, she'd been trapped in darkness. The warm light felt good on her. But something was wrong about this place. It was too quiet—way to quiet. There were no reporters or photographers. There were no cars were parked outside their house. Only her mother's car was in the drive way. The silence spooked her a bit because, whenever there was silence, she believed that something terrible might have happened. That's how it had always been.

But not today. This was a new day. She wasn't going to let anything bad happen on this day. She would be sure of that. She missed everyone. She wanted to see everyone. She wanted to have one of their weird celebrations that always made her laugh.

The sunshine greeted her and welcomed her home as she made her way to the house. She held on to Joey's hand and didn't let go until they got to the front door. She acted as if someone might come up and snatch him away from her again. *Why am I acting like this? It's all over,* she told herself. *Things will go back to normal. No, not normal. Things will never be the same. I have changed. I am a different person now. I am my old self, but also a new person.*

Finally, she opened the door. They walked inside. The house was quiet also. But then they heard weeping, almost silent weeping. They could barely hear it. It sounded familiar. They had heard it when their dad died. It had been nonstop, but it had not been a seeking-attention kind of crying. It was their mother. She was crying. Following the sounds, they walked into the living room. There was her mother, sitting on a pink couch in the middle of the room. Their grandparents sat beside her, trying to comfort her. Rena and Joey's mother covered her face with her hands. Her hair was wet and tangled and looked as if she hasn't brushed it in days. "I just don't know what could have happened," she said, still covering her face. "I gave them a lot of attention. Why would they want to leave?"

Rena felt guilty. How could she have just left everyone? How could she have had the selfish thought of leaving everyone to stay with Zidika when they all wanted to see her and wanted her home? They were all waiting for her and Joey. She thought she'd understood what they would have felt without them, but she hadn't truly understand. She hadn't understood anything, but now she did. She wanted to run to her mother and tell her that everything was all right, that none of this was her fault, that she was a great mother, and that she shouldn't change anything about herself. Even though sometimes she would be gone for long periods of time, she was still a great mother and friend. Rena wanted her mother to know that it was all not her mother's fault, but Rena's.

But Rena just stood there, not moving an inch. She leaned against the frame of the open door and felt tears falling. Her mother lifted her head. Her eyes were red and puffy, a waterfall of tears still fell, and her checks were red and rosy. Her entire face was red from crying. "I just don't—" then she stopped herself when she saw them standing at the door. "Rena! Joey! I'm not just imagining this, am I? You see them too?" she said, turning to Rena's grandmother. She nodded. "My darlings!" she said. She stood and held her arms out.

"Mother!" Rena said, springing into a run. Joey followed after her. They both ran into their mother's arms. She hugged them tightly and they did the same.

"My kids!"

"Mother!" They both cried in their mother's arms.

"You don't know how much I missed you!"

"You don't know how much we missed *you!*" they both said. Rena didn't realize how much she had missed everything until she got back home. She was glad she was finally home.

Their mother pulled away from them and looked at them. Her eyes and cheeks were still puffy. "Now, you two, tell me where have you been. I have been worried sick since I got a call from school saying that you hadn't arrived. I left work immediately."

"You haven't been at your job?"

"How could I think of modeling when my two kids are missing? You guys mean everything to me! I am so blessed to have you both in my life. The police have been searching. I got the newspapers involved. I even put up posters! I told everybody I knew to search for you. But no one could find you. Where did you go?"

"A secret place, Mother," Joey said.

Rena gave him a look and then looked at her mom. "Yeah, something like that. Let's just say we went hiking."

Her mother gave her a confused look. "Usually you roll your eyes and walk away to try and avoid the subject as much as possible," she said. "What happened?" She shook her head. "It doesn't matter. At least I have my two kids back." She hugged them again. "Now get upstairs and clean yourselves up. Look at you two! You are filthy!"

Rena hadn't noticed, but she had to agree that she needed to take a long shower and clean herself up. She also needed to put on some clean and fresh good-smelling clothes. Rena and Joey both ran upstairs.

After her long shower, Rena came downstairs, drying her hair with a fluffy towel. She walked into the kitchen, and her eyes widened. "Wow, Mom! What happened in here? It looks like you're making dinner for the king! Plus," she said as she sniffed the air, "it smells like you burned something."

"Well, how can I not go all out tonight? I finally have my two kids home after they disappeared for several months." She smiled and then turned back to the soup she was making. She almost freaked out as she was about to overcook it. She quickly tuned the stove off, grabbed the pot of soup, and ran to the sink. Quickly she poured it out before it exploded, because in that kitchen, if something got overcooked, almost every time it exploded. Rena laughed as she watched her mother. Something like this always happened to her, and it was funny to finally see it again. It was good to be home.

***

"Rena, get ready for school. It's your first day back since ..." Rena's mother stopped talking. In a moment, she spoke again. "Just get ready. I don't want you to be late."

Rena was excited to go back to school, but also, deep inside, she didn't want to. She didn't want people to pay too much attention over the fact that she was finally back. Of course, she liked the attention, but sometimes it could go too far. She didn't want the whole school creating a party welcoming her back. At least she didn't think she wanted that.

She walked out of her room wearing blue jeans and a pink shirt that said "rock star." She saw Joey heading downstairs and decided to join him. When she walked outside, only one reporter and photographer stood at the front door. Rena was amazed that there weren't more trying to take pictures of their sudden return. As she walked outside, the reporter and photographer walked up to her. Rena didn't mind, but for right now she just wanted to be alone. She couldn't just tell them that; she knew that, in the end, they still wouldn't leave her alone.

"Hello, Rena. May we ask you a few questions?"

"Huh? Sure, but make it quick because I don't want to be late for class." She looked at her watch. She wondered where Joey had run off to, but remembered he had a bus to catch. The photographer took one picture of her, and the flash surprised Rena.

"How is it that you and your brother were able to disappear for a few months without anyone being able to find you?"

Rena purposely acted as if she didn't want to answer. The photographer understood and told the reporter to go on with the next question. "Would you mind coming with us for a while?"

Rena nodded and followed. She got in their car, and they drove her to a place she knew quite well. "What are we doing at my mother's job?"

The reporter turned to face her. "You'll see," he said, smiling. Then he turned his attention back to the road.

When the car stopped, Rena jumped out. "Hey, look, I don't know why you brought me here. But I need you to take me back. My classes are about to start."

"Oh, I don't think you need to worry about your classes."

"What?"

"Follow us, Rena." Rena refused at first, but then gave in and did as she was told. When they entered the building, she was surprised to see all her classmates standing under a sign that said, Welcome Back! Rena was delighted. She had expected something like this to happen, but for some reason she didn't think they would do something like this! She never dreamed they would actually create a party at her mother's workplace. She thought maybe they would make a small party in one of the classrooms at school. But this was awesome! Her brother and his classmates were there as well.

"What's all this?" Rena asked her mom when she came up to her.

"Birthday party and welcome home party! We never did celebrate your birthday, so Joey came up with the idea to have a party here."

"At your work?"

"Well, duh … so that you can …" Without any more explanation, she led Rena through the crowd to the back of the building to the photo studio. Rena was surprised at what she saw. An entire Japanese city had been constructed as a backdrop It reminded Rena of Tokyo. People were walking around dressed in kimonos, and trees drenched in cherry blossoms were scattered everywhere.

"Oh, my gosh! You did all this for me?"

"I know how much you love the Japanese culture," said her mother. "Since I never had my photo shoot, I thought I would create one so we could both be in it."

"Thank you," Rena said as she hugged her mother. She was overjoyed. Finally things were going her way.

"Go talk with your friends while I'll get everything ready."

Rena nodded and ran, all excited, to see her three best friends. She knew that they would be happy and excited to see her too. All three of them were waiting for her to come back from the studio. Rena pushed through the crowd. When she saw them, she was overjoyed, and she ran up to them and hugged all three of them. "I can't believe you guys came! I can't believe how happy I am to see you—everybody."

"Wow, Rena, what's up with the sudden change?" said her friend who had the brightly colored curls. She had noticed a change in Rena right away, and was a little surprised to see the new Rena. But it was still Rena, her best friend, and she would love her and understand her even if she had changed.

"Oh, it doesn't matter because we still love you," said her friend who had dark short hair.

Inside Rena felt her heart brighten just a little more. Rena turned to greet some other friends. After she finished talking with everyone, she spotted Joey among the crowd. She walked up to him. "Joey, thank you for all this."

"No, thank you for all that you did for me, Rena." They hugged each other.

"So, you remember?"

"No, but Celesta told me."

Rena was shocked to hear that, but it really didn't matter. If it didn't bother Joey, then it was all right with her. Rena smiled at Joey. "You'll always be my dearest brother."

"And you will always be my older sister!"

"Okay, everybody!" A loud voice quieted the crowd. Everyone turned around to see where the voice was coming from. It was coming from a loud speaker, but they couldn't see the person speaking. "Everything is ready. You can come inside." People didn't hesitate to rush into the room. When they arrived, they were all amazed at how beautiful Rena's mother looked. She wore a bright-green kimono with dark stripes. Her hair was tied up with red ribbons.

"Rena, come here." Rena felt embarrassed because all her school friends were watching. Because everyone was staring and all eyes were on her, she was the center of attention. She walked up to her mother, and they both went inside the dressing room. After a few minutes, Rena came out wearing a dark-pink kimono with hot-pink stripes, and her hair was also tied with red ribbons. Like mother, like daughter. They both were stunning.

Rena enjoyed the rest of the day, and she was amazed at how everything turned out. This was the best birthday ever. When they came home from the party, Rena waited for the rest of the day for the pictures to arrive. When they arrived a few hours later, Rena immediately opened the package. Inside was the kimono she had worn and the decorations they had used in her hair. These were a gift from the manager. When she looked at the pictures, she barely recognized herself, but not because of what she wore. Rather, she realized that she looked like a totally different person—beautiful on the inside as well as the outside.

She put her favorite picture in a beautiful frame and put it on her desk where she could always look at it. She framed another picture—of her and her mom—and hung it above her bed. Everything was going to be okay from that day on.

CHAPTER 30

Will He Come Back?

· ·

A month had passed, and Rena had found herself in the shed looking at the mirror every single day. She held the chain Zidika had given her with both hands and squeezed the leaf charm tightly. Then she looked at the silver leaf. It looked familiar, but she couldn't quite remember where she might have seen it. She did experience a blurry image of a boy with white hair. It was hard to tell if she knew this boy because she couldn't quite remember what he looked like. But she did remember meeting this boy at the park and ... Wait! She remembered this silver chain with the leaf charm. She'd seen it around that boy's neck! That was what had brought them together—when she first saw the necklace, she had been amazed by it, and she had asked the kid a lot of questions about it. That was how their friendship had begun.

Zidika has given her this necklace, and if that little boy she had met at the park had worn it, then he must have been Zidika! Wow! That explained a lot.

She twisted the symbol on the mirror so it would show her the other world. She stared at it for a few seconds before she turned the symbol back again. Then she stared at her reflection. After her father died, she didn't go to the park for a long time. When she did finally did return, she wanted to see that boy, but he was not there. She remembered how upset she had been. She had actually cried for a long time. Maybe that was part of the reason she had locked herself up—so she could forget her feelings about him so his loss wouldn't sting her and hurt her anymore.

If Zidika was really that childhood friend she had met three years ago, then would mean … Her thoughts were interrupted when she heard someone coming, and she tuned to see who it was. It was her mother. "Rena, honey, are you okay?" She walked up to her.

Rena sighed. "Yeah, in a way I am."

"Are you sure? Because I have found you here several times staring at this old mirror looking so sad and worried. Are you sure you're okay?"

"Yes, Mother, I am." She tried to force a smile. "Just waiting for someone," she said, and she walked away.

CHAPTER 31

You're Back!

· · · · · · · · · · · · ·

When Rena got back from the shed, she quickly got her backpack and headed out to the bus stop. She hadn't wanted to ride the taxi anymore, so her mom had told the taxi company not to come anymore.

When the school bell rang, announcing the end of the school day, Rena walked outside talking and laughing with her friends. They were all talking about a prank that some of the students had pulled on the coach, and they thought it was hilarious. "Who's that hot guy standing over there?" One of her friends nudged her, encouraging her to look where she was pointing.

Rena immediately stopped when she saw him—a handsome, cute boy with slightly long white hair.

"Does he go to this school?" asked another of her friends.

"No, he's kinda not from here," Rena said slowly, almost not believing it was him.

"Hey, Rena, do you know him?" She didn't answer. She only stood there, frozen, her eyes wide open. She was overjoyed to see him, but also angry that he hadn't told her. Why hadn't he told her? It was only today that she realized he was actually from the future—from her world.

Soon her anger evaporated. Everything around her disappeared, and she no longer cared about the outside world, what was happening around her.

Her eyes locked with his. All her focus was on him. She was happy to see him. She was happier to see him than she had been to see anyone in entire life. She had known that he would come. She had hoped that he would. Tears escaped from her eyes and slithered down her cheeks. Her mind drifted off as she remembered precious moments with him.

For two minutes, Rena did not move. Everything around her stood still. It was as if they were the only two people in the world. Nothing mattered, not anymore, not at that moment. Then she started running as fast as her feet could carry her. She leaped into his arms. The warmth of his jacket surrounded her. His arms went around her waist. She buried her face in his jacket, and she cried happy tears.

Zidika squeezed her more tightly. She felt warm, her skin was soft, and she smelled good. They both stood hugging each other before Rena's dark eyes stared into his. "Why didn't tell me you could travel through the mirror?" she said with a frown.

"I wanted to surprise you." He sweetly smiled at her, his eyes dancing in happiness.

"You jerk! I was so worried that I would never get to see you again!" She cried fake tears and tore herself away from him. "You made me wait for a month!" she said, crossing her arms.

"Rena," he said in a gentle voice. His soft amber eyes stared at her. She could tell that he was happy to see her. He was happier than he had ever been to see anyone.

Rena felt lost in his eyes. The look he gave her melted her away. She felt blown away by his smile. As he walked close to her, Rena broke away from her daydream. She pushed herself away from him, smiling thinking of something. "You want me? You've got to catch me!" she yelled. And she started running away. She wanted to grab her backpack, but there wouldn't be enough time so she just left it.

Zidika watched her as she ran. He smiled and ran after her. When he finally caught up to her, he took her hand and pulled her close to him, locking his lips with hers.

Her mind was all foggy. She closed her eyes to hold back the tingly sensation. *Is this how it feels to kiss someone? Someone you truly love? It's like sparks flying!* Her heart pounded loudly inside her chest. It skipped a few beats when he pushed her back against a tree. Her heart was racing. It must have been awkward with all her friends staring, but Zidika didn't seem to notice, so she didn't care.

CHAPTER 32

Not the Last

. . . .

"So, are you guys, like, dating now?" said her friend with the short brown hair.

This made Rena blush. "Yeah, you could say that," she said as the four friends walked home together. Soon the girl who had asked the question said she needed to do something, so she left. The other two walked home with Rena.

As they walked, Rena remembered what Zidika had told her before she left.

> "Well, Rena," Zidika said, "I know we just met after a month of separation, but I'm sorry to tell you this."

> Rena stopped him. She nodded as if she understood and knew what he was going to say next. "You want to leave to go find your parents, family members, and friends. I understand that. You must really miss them. I've realized how much I miss mine, and I've been gone for only a few months. But you have been gone for three years! I understand how you must feel, and they will be happy to see you."

> "So, you cool?"

"Yeah, I'm cool." They hugged each other one last time.

"Rena, I will miss you."

"And I will miss you."

"You do know we aren't going to be apart for long, right?"

"I know," she said, trying not to think about how long they would be apart for the second time.

"No, I mean really. I remember this place. The park I used to go is about forty minutes away, so that means my folks live an hour and thirty minutes away."

"That's great!" Rena smiled, remembering the park. But before he left, Rena asked him something. "Zidika, how did you end up going through the mirror and not remembering anything?"

Zidika thought for bit. "Because it was just hard to deal with." And he didn't tell her more than that. He left Rena wondering what he could have meant.

Rena held the leaf necklace with both her hands tightly. She felt the warm spring breeze blow. It tickled her skin. She watched as her friends' hair went flying and shone so brightly and beautifully as the bright warm sun rays of spring made the day all around them seem perfect. It made the roses seem more beautiful and smell their best.

Rena felt relieved that she wouldn't have to stay separated from Zidika for too long. The wind sent her hair flying, and she looked up at the sky and smiled. She knew the reason for her journey to the past.

Printed in the United States
By Bookmasters